SHARON M. DRAPER

PANIC

 Atheneum Books for Young Readers
NEW YORK LONDON TORONTO SYDNEY NEW DELHI

ATHENEUM BOOKS FOR YOUNG READERS
An imprint of Simon & Schuster Children's Publishing Division
1230 Avenue of the Americas, New York, New York 10020
This book is a work of fiction. Any references to historical events, real
people, or real places are used fictitiously. Other names, characters,
places, and events are products of the author's imagination, and any
resemblance to actual events or places or persons, living or dead, is
entirely coincidental.
Copyright © 2013 by Sharon M. Draper

ATHENEUM BOOKS FOR YOUNG READERS is a registered trademark of
Simon & Schuster, Inc.
Atheneum logo is a trademark of Simon & Schuster, Inc.
For information about special discounts for bulk purchases, please
contact Simon & Schuster Special Sales at 1-866-506-1949 or
business@simonandschuster.com.
The Simon & Schuster Speakers Bureau can bring authors to your
live event. For more information or to book an event, contact the
Simon & Schuster Speakers Bureau at 1-866-248-3049 or visit our
website at www.simonspeakers.com.
Book design by Debra Sfetsios-Conover
The text for this book is set in New Baskerville.
Manufactured in the United States of America
First Edition
10 9 8 7 6 5 4 3 2 1
Library of Congress Cataloging-in-Publication Data
Draper, Sharon M. (Sharon Mills)
Panic / Sharon M. Draper.—1st ed.
p. cm.
Summary: As rehearsals begin for the ballet version of *Peter Pan*, the teenaged members of an Ohio
dance troupe lose their focus when one of their own goes missing.
ISBN 978-1-4424-0896-8
ISBN 978-1-4424-0898-2 (eBook)
[1. Dance—Fiction. 2. Kidnapping—Fiction. 3. Sexual abuse—Fiction. 4. African Americans—
Fiction.] I. Title.
PZ7.D78325Pan 2013
[Fic]—dc23
2012016339

This book is dedicated to dancers everywhere,
but especially to Miss Crystal and the wonderful students
of Kinetic Expressions Dance Academy
in Daytona Beach, Florida
(http://www.facebook.com/KEDAdance)

Acknowledgments

Many thanks to the following:
All the KEDA families who support their children
as they learn and grow through dance.
All the KEDA students who work so hard and perform
so beautifully.
Yes, this book is about you. No, that character is not you.
For real!

To my family who supports me as I work to do what I do:
Crystal
Damon and Mary
Larry Draper
Cory and Wendy.

And a special shout out to
Diane Swirka.

Also, please be aware of the dangers of teen dating abuse
as well as predators who stalk our children. I found these websites
to be helpful and informative:

http://www.ctcadv.org/WhatisDomesticViolence/
WhatisTeenDatingViolence/tabid/169/Default.aspx

http://www.state.gov/j/tip/rls/tiprpt/2010

http://klaaskids.org

http://www.publicsafety.ohio.gov/links/cjs0034.pdf

1

JUSTIN, *Friday, April 12   4 p.m.*

"'Proud and insolent youth,' said Hook, 'prepare to meet thy doom.'

"'Dark and sinister man,' Peter answered, 'have at thee.'"

—from *Peter Pan*

"Hey, dance boy!"

Sixteen-year-old Justin Braddock, wearing his favorite Timberland boots, tromped down the rain-slicked sidewalk, book bag slung over his left shoulder, heading to the bus stop. He did not turn around—he knew who trailed behind him.

"You heard me, dancing queen! Don't be tiptoeing away, now."

Justin sighed. Another fight.

Zac Patterson, the wrestling team's "sultan of the slam," was known to brandish both his biceps and equally massive ego. He yelled louder. "What up, fag!"

"Swish!" added Ben Bones. Justin knew Bones would be hovering just a few steps behind Zac, safe like a shadow.

Justin tried to ignore the idiots behind him. Guys had been teasing him for years, ever since he started taking dance lessons. He was as tall as Zac, more muscled than Bones. But most guys seemed clueless about the athletic skills required for the leaps and lifts he had mastered. And none of them knew how much he loved it.

"Look how he twitches those hips!" Zac jeered.

Justin wondered, amused, why Zac was so interested in his butt.

"Got your shiny pink toe shoes stuffed in that bag? Who braids your hair—yo mama?" Bones asked, laughing loudly with Zac.

"Your mama wears a tutu too!" Zac and Bones hooted with laughter.

Justin stopped walking. He tossed his backpack on the ground and spun around. "Don't you talk about my mother!" he hissed. A surge of rage and sorrow coursed through him. His mother had died less than a year before, and it felt like yesterday. It felt like forever.

"Your mama so stupid, she tried to put her M&M's in alphabetical order!" Bones sniped, still standing safely behind Zac.

Justin was not in a mood to play the dozens. Not today. Not ever. Not about his mom.

"Your mama twice the man you are," Zac sneered.

Nope.

Not today.

Justin did not hesitate. He wheeled around, tightened his right fist, then, with a *whump*, he planted a direct blow to the center of Zac's gut.

Zac, all two hundred pounds of him, crumpled in a heap on the sidewalk. "Oomph," he managed to mumble.

Bones, looking terrified, placed both his hands in a strategic position to protect himself, but Justin just glared at him.

"Dance with *that*!" Justin said as he picked up his pack. He continued down the street and did not look back.

2

JUSTIN, *Friday, April 12   5 p.m.*

". . . who cuts whistles out of the trees and dances ecstatically to his own tunes."
—from *Peter Pan*

Justin stepped nimbly off the bus, half a block away from the Crystal Pointe Dance Academy. He came here almost every day after school, and the place felt like a second home. Roomy and airy, done up in tones of red and black and white, it housed well over a hundred students—most of them girls.

He paused in the parking lot as a dark maroon Cadillac Escalade truck pulled in. In it was Layla Ridgewood, who was dropped off every day by her boyfriend, Donovan.

Donovan Beaudry rolled his window down; ear-splittingly loud rap music exploded from the truck's custom-installed sound gear. The SUV rolled on twenty-four-inch dubs and sported a shiny set of Sprewells that Justin knew cost around $2,000 a set. The hubcaps continued to spin even after the car came to a stop. He didn't even want to think about how Donovan could have paid for all that.

Donovan kept his head shaved bald, probably to show off the tattoos on his neck, Justin figured. Another tat covered his entire left arm, spelling out "Layla" in script lettering. He glanced at Justin, coughed, then spit in his direction.

Justin glanced at him coolly. He didn't move. He and Donovan had once been best friends. In elementary school they'd played soldiers outside and video games inside.

But by their early teens Donny started to change. He was a year older, and when he got to middle school, he started to hang out with the boys who skipped classes and sold their mothers' prescription pills behind the gym. By the time Justin got to sixth grade, the two had grown apart.

"'Sup?" Donovan said lazily.

"Just chillin'," Justin replied.

"Still playin' ballerina with the girls every day? There's somethin' just messed up with that, man."

"So you say."

"Why can't you play football or basketball like a real dude?" Donovan's voice was filled with scorn.

"I don't see *you* wearin' cleats and shoulder pads," Justin countered.

"I'm a lover, man. Ain't got time for sweatin' on some football field. But if that's what I wanted to do, I'd be the best man on the team, not some sissy who dances with girls."

Justin smiled. "Dude, for four hours every day I get to hang with a room full of shorties dressed in shorts and tights and leotards. *You* the one who don't get it, man. I'm just swagged out like that!"

Donovan pointed a finger at Justin. "Just make sure you keep away from my Layla. She comes here to dance, not to be felt up by you."

Justin flexed his forearms. "I got mad respect for Layla—and all the girls here."

"You cross the line, I'll make you suffer. You got that?" Donovan spat out the window again, then pulled Layla toward him and kissed her roughly.

When she got out of the car, Layla swiped her hand across her mouth, then waved cheerfully as Donovan gunned the engine and drove away. He didn't wave back.

"Hey, Justin," Layla said. "You know, you gotta just ignore Donny. He's all smoke."

"Yeah, I know." He paused, then went for it. "But I wonder if you do."

Layla's eyes went flat for a second; she swallowed and then opened her mouth to answer, quickly changing the subject. "How was school today?" They both went to Broadway High, where Layla was a sophomore and Justin was a junior.

"Same old. What's up with you?"

"Chillaxin'. Glad to get here so I can stretch out some of my stress."

"Girl, what you got to be stressed about? The show tomorrow? Donovan?" Justin asked as they walked to the front door of the studio.

"Donny's great, but you know—stuff at home, stuff at school. This is the only place where I feel like I can really kick it. And OMG, the show is gonna be off the chain!"

"I feel ya."

Justin pulled open the heavy red wooden doors for her and breathed in happily. Layla was right. Music played softly from speakers in the ceiling. To the left was the Crystal Café, a cozy little room with vending machines, a microwave, and an odd assortment of tables and chairs to lounge in. Students came in from school and gobbled whatever was available that week.

"I wonder if the Wi-Fi is up," Layla mused as she got a diet cola and granola bar from the machines.

Justin got out his iPad and checked. "Yep. Miss Ginger musta got it fixed. You're free to update your Facebook status to 'Still lockin' lips with Donovan!'"

She looked at him, sipped her soda, then said, "What? You jealous?"

"He's a lucky man," Justin admitted. "I just don't think he realizes what a good thing he's got."

Layla looked away. "I think he knows. I just hope he remembers."

Justin wasn't exactly sure what *that* meant, but he kept his face a mask and headed for the main dance room. He cued up "Beat It" by Michael Jackson. Yeah, it was old, but it was timeless. He turned the music up as loud as it would go and let it wash over him as he pulled off his shirt and his shoes. Wearing only sweatpants, he began to move to the rhythms that pounded around him. He stretched for a few moments, then he began to spin. He bounded. He leaped. He did coffee grinders and helicopters, body glides and freezes.

He'd started as a B-boy dancer, popping and locking for fun in his living room, showing off for his parents as he spun on his head or balanced on his arms. But at the studio he'd discovered jazz dance styles, modern, and even ballet. He was amazed how easily each form had come to him. It was like sampling new flavors of candy, each bubbling to its own soundtrack.

Covered with sweat and breathing hard, Justin finally stopped when he realized several students were standing by the mirrors, watching him. A couple of them clapped.

"Great job, Justin," Miss Ginger called out as she breezed into the room. She tossed him a towel. Lithe and muscular, she could outdance most of the students who attended her studio, even though she had to be at least forty years old. Her frizzy brown-gray hair framed her face like a halo.

"Thanks, Miss Ginger. I was just warming up." He wiped his face and glanced back at Layla. She was busily texting—*Probably Donovan,* he thought.

"Have you posted the cast for *Peter Pan* yet?" Diamond Landers asked the teacher. Tryouts had been held two days ago for the highlight of the year—the June full-company dance adaptation of a major Broadway show.

"You can find the list online tonight," Miss Ginger replied. "I am *so* looking forward to working with you guys—it's going to be awesome!"

"Any hints?" Diamond asked, teasing. Justin knew she really wanted the lead in that show—the part of Wendy.

"You know me better than that, Diamond," Miss Ginger said, her voice stern but kind.

"I'm just so amped up!" Diamond said, doing a couple of piqué turns across the floor.

"First things first," Miss Ginger told her. "We've got to get through our spring showcase, which is *tomorrow*!"

"I'm just sayin' . . . ," Diamond said to anyone who was listening as she pretended to float across the floor to her place on the barre. She twirled in place, then grinned at Justin, who just shook his head in bemusement.

Miss Ginger called the class to order, and the rest of the students trickled in from the café, the dressing rooms, and the lounge. She plugged her iPod into the speakers, chose a song, and gave a clap, "Let's begin. We have a performance in less than twenty-four hours, and we have so much to do."

Justin exhaled and then smiled to himself. *It doesn't get better than this.*

CRYSTAL POINTE DANCE ACADEMY
CAST LIST FOR *PETER PAN*

Wendy Darling	Layla Ridgewood
Peter Pan	Jillian Aylor
Tiger Lily	Mercedes Ford
John Darling	Tara Picassa
Michael Darling	Tina Picassa
Captain Hook	Justin Braddock
Smee the Pirate	Diamond Landers
Nana the Dog	Zizi Cho
Tock the Crocodile	Zizi Cho
Tinker Bell	Elizabeth Flemming
Tink's Helpers	Jr. Company dancers
The Lost Boys	Company dancers
Pirates	Company dancers
Indians	Company dancers

Posted Friday, April 12

3

DIAMOND, *Saturday, April 13   2 p.m.*

"All are keeping a sharp look-out in front, but none suspects that
the danger may be creeping up from behind."
—from *Peter Pan*

"We're swingin' by the mall to get new tights for tonight's
performance, Mom," Diamond yelled up the stairs.

"Didn't I just buy you tights last week?" her mother
answered as she leaned over the railing.

"Those were *pink* tights, Mom. I need beige ones.
Pink is just for ballet!"

Mrs. Landers threw her hands up in frustration and

came downtairs. "I can't keep up with you kids and your dance stuff. So when do you need the red tights?"

"Those were for that little show we did at the middle school last week. Don't you remember?" Diamond looked at her friend Mercedes Ford, who grinned at the nearly identical "mom conversations" they both were forced to endure before they left the house.

"Now tell me again what time the show starts and where it's going to be," Diamond's mother said.

Diamond sighed. "Seven thirty, Mom. Miss Ginger is using Broadway High's auditorium for this performance, remember? You got the tickets?"

"I got the tickets. Shasta and Dad and I will be there, right up front."

"Remember, this is just the spring showcase—I don't have a very big part tonight. And I'm in the back row."

"I don't care. I simply love watching you dance, even if you're only onstage for a hot minute," her mother said, smoothing Diamond's curly brown hair and adjusting her pink flowing cover-up so her bra straps didn't show. "You know I wouldn't miss this."

"Can I come to the mall with you?" Diamond's nine-year-old sister, Shasta, asked, popping in from the kitchen. She was busy peeling a banana.

"Sorry, Shasta-blasta. Not this time. We've got rehearsal, and this show is just for the older kids. I'll see you after the performance, with Mom and Dad, okay?" Diamond told her.

"Is Justin in the show?" Shasta asked.

"Well, yeah. Duh! He's the only advanced male in our

studio right now. He's, like, vital. Who else can do duos and lifts and stuff?"

"He's cute," Shasta said with a giggle, stuffing half the banana into her mouth.

"He's sixteen!"

"So?" Shasta tossed the peel in the trash and put her hands on her hips.

"So you better behave, young lady," Mrs. Landers said with a laugh.

"Don't forget, banana breath, you'll *be* in the next show!" Diamond reminded her. "I am so hyped for *Peter Pan*. Me and you will be together for every single rehearsal and every single performance."

"That's not till June," Shasta groaned as she gulped down the fruit. "I need to hang with you so I can learn all the juicy stuff about dance." She twirled clumsily, stumbled, and caught a teetering lamp just before it toppled over. "Sorry, Mom," she said as she continued to whirl around the sofa and chairs. Her sneakers blinked and sparkled with every step.

Diamond laughed. "There's no juicy stuff, Shasta, unless you count the sweat."

"Ick!" Shasta flopped down on the sofa. "Hey! Did Miss Ginger post the parts yet? What did I get?"

"Yeah, she posted them online last night," Mercedes told her.

"Really? The list is up? Why didn't you tell me?" Diamond's mother asked. "What part did you get, sweetie?"

Diamond shrugged. "I didn't get the role of Wendy like I wanted."

"*Any* part you play makes me proud," her mother said.

"Yeah. Well, glad *you're* proud. I get to be Smee the pirate." She paused, looking at the floor. "That totally sucks."

Mrs. Landers pulled Diamond close. "You are my star, Diamond," she whispered into her ear. "Never forget that. And you will be the best Smee ever."

Diamond leaned into the hug and let her mom smooth her hair.

Shasta, up again and now trying to balance on her toes, interrupted. "What part did I get? Can I be Tinker Bell? I'm little enough."

Diamond got down on her knees, eye level with her sister. "No, but you can be one of Tinker Bell's assistants!"

"Do I get a cute costume?" Shasta asked warily.

"I think all the little Tinks get costumes that light up!"

Shasta did a happy little wiggle. "Awesome! So let me come with you to the mall so I can get some sparkly tights."

"You'd have holes in them by the time we do that show." Diamond laughed. "You've got plenty of time to get your costume together and tons of rehearsals before that."

"Do I get a magic wand?"

"Probably. I'll ask Miss Ginger."

"I want a purple one!" Shasta insisted. "Pinkie promise." She held out the little finger of her right hand.

Diamond hooked her finger to her sister's tiny one. "I'll do my best."

Appeased for the moment, Shasta headed back to the kitchen.

"Mom, we better go," Diamond said. "Miss Ginger will kill us if we're late for rehearsal."

"You be careful driving, Mercedes," Mrs. Landers said, glancing out the window. "It's pouring rain out there."

"I will. I promise," Mercedes replied. "I got my driver's license on a rainy day," she added, "so I'm cool."

Mrs. Landers continued to look worried. "And no texting while you drive. You don't need to be on your phone at all until you get to the mall."

"You got it, Mrs. L. No cell at all. We'll just make a quick stop at the mall, and we'll call you when we get to the school."

"Bye, Mom. Love you! We'll see you there!" Diamond yelled as she grabbed her hot pink dance bag and headed out the door.

"Bye, girls. Dance well. Can't wait to see the showcase."

Diamond slammed the door and laughed out loud. "My mother is a trip! I swear!"

"She's just doin' her thing. Don't sweat it." Mercedes, pulling the hood of her Cincinnati Reds sweatshirt over her head, ran with Diamond, dodging raindrops, to her car.

"Too bad you don't get to drive a car as cool as your name," Diamond said as she climbed into the sturdy blue 2004 Ford Focus. "Your ride is messed up."

"Hey, my name *is* my car—no matter what I drive!" Mercedes replied with a smirk. "Today I drive my last name. But a Mercedes waits for me in my future." She checked her hair in the rearview mirror, nodding with approval. Slicked back and sprayed into a bun, not a strand was out of place.

"At least you got a car." Diamond sighed. "I can't wait until I get my license. One more year! I'm so sick of my mom driving me everywhere, I could scream." She glanced at Mercedes' sleek black hair. Her own curls were tousled and unruly. It took practically a whole can of hair spray to make hers behave on performance nights.

"I bet your mother is just as sick of being your driver. My mom can't dance worth nuthin', and she jumped around the house like a hoochie-coochie girl when I got my license."

"I'm glad I didn't have to see that," Diamond said with a laugh, buckling her seat belt.

Mercedes turned the radio up. The windshield wipers seemed to move to the music.

"Hey, text Steve for me, will ya?" Mercedes asked. "Remind him to bring my chocolate bars to the back-stage door."

"Can't you just get some from the mall?" Diamond asked her as she took out her phone.

"Yeah, but candy from Steve tastes *so* much better," Mercedes said, licking her lips.

"You're a mess, girl." But Diamond tapped in the message. Steve texted back in seconds. "He said he'd bring the candy to his favorite chocolate bunny. Oh, gag me now!"

"He texts me every single morning," Mercedes said happily.

"Yeah, I know. It's so sweet I can't stand it."

"You want to hear what he sent this morning?"

"I don't know—do I? My head might explode."

"He said, 'Morning, butterfly. Hope you slept well.'

16

Then he sent me a link to Mariah Carey's old song 'Butterfly.'"

"I'm 'bout to choke up in here!"

Mercedes' and Diamond's cell phones then beeped at the same time.

"Who's double-texting?" Mercedes mused.

"Duh. Miss Ginger, reminding us not to be late." Diamond held up both phones, which blinked the same message.

"Text her back on both phones and tell her we're on our way. We never shoulda taught that woman technology!"

"Oh, man." Diamond groaned as she glanced at the bars at the top of her phone. "My phone's about to die, and I forgot my charger."

"I think Miss Ginger has a charger at the studio that will fit," Mercedes said. "It's probably one you left there! You go through chargers like Shasta goes through Popsicles!"

"True that."

Mercedes upped the volume on the radio and sang along whenever a favorite song came on. During a commercial, though, Mercedes turned off the radio. She glanced at Diamond a few times, and finally asked, "So, are you upset about not getting the part of Wendy in *Peter Pan*? You've been kinda quiet about it."

Diamond sighed. "I'm glad Layla got it. She works really hard, and I guess she deserves it. But it's still a bummer. I've never had a lead in any of Miss Ginger's shows. I'm starting to think . . . well . . . that I'm just not good enough."

"Oh, you're good enough, girlfriend. Maybe Miss

Ginger is saving you for a lead in next year's show. I heard she's doing *Cinderella*." Mercedes drove in silence for a moment.

"Yeah, but to just be a stupid pirate . . ." She paused.

"But he's the main one after Hook—you get to be onstage a lot," Mercedes said encouragingly.

"Big fat whoop."

"Jillian will be pretty good as Peter Pan," Mercedes continued.

"I figured that role would go to her. I'd never tell her, but she's probably our best dancer."

"I feel ya. She's flat-chested and skinny and perfect for that part. She's probably texting and tweeting to the world that she got the lead role."

Diamond grunted. "Yeah, but dressed like a boy. She can have it."

Mercedes turned the corner to the mall. "Still, it's gonna be a good show—Miss Ginger always turns it out. Justin will be dynamite as Captain Hook."

"What about you?" Diamond asked. "Are you cool with Tiger Lily?"

"For real, I'm geeked. It's the part I wanted—I'm dying to do that insane fight scene with the pirates. I can't wait for rehearsals to start!"

"I guess," Diamond agreed, but she wished she felt as excited as Mercedes sounded.

Mercedes, mimicking their teacher's grab-your-guts-and-stand-up-straight voice, said, "All performance experience is good for the soul!"

Diamond cracked up, nodding. "Park by the back

entrance," she suggested. "It's closer to the dance store."

"And the food court. I'm desperate for a slice!"

"Me too," Diamond said, grabbing her dance bag as they headed inside. The rain had slowed to a drizzle.

"Why don't you just leave that in the car?" Mercedes asked.

"I don't care if somebody steals my school bag," Diamond said, slinging it over her shoulder. "Actually, I hope they do! But my dance bag is my life. It's like I can't breathe without it."

"You crazy."

They hit C'est La Danse first. Owned by a woman who had been a dancer in Paris, it was like heaven to Diamond and Mercedes. They could find their favorite Capezio tights and Sansha shoes, plus dance bags, warm-ups, even sparkle-studded earrings and key chains designed to look like ballet slippers.

"Hey, Madame Jolie." They'd been in the store so often that the owner knew them by name.

"Welcome back, *mes cheries*. What do you need on this rainy day?"

"We need nude tights—size adult medium," Diamond said.

"Ah, *oui*," she said. "Of course. And have you seen these new leotards with the cutout backs?" Madame Jolie asked, pointing to a display. "*C'est très* sexy!"

"Oh, that's what's up! I gotta try this red one on," Mercedes said excitedly.

Diamond checked her watch. "Look, girl, you got a weakness, but I'm starving, and we're gonna be late for rehearsal. Meet me at the food court in ten."

"Gotcha. Get me a plain cheese slice, okay? I'll eat it in the car." Mercedes was already disappearing into the tiny dressing room.

Diamond paid for her tights and stuffed them into her ballet bag. Slinging it back over her shoulder, she waved good-bye to Madame Jolie and headed out.

4

DIAMOND, *Saturday, April 13   2:30 p.m.*

"Our last glimpse of her shows her at the window,

watching them receding into the sky until they were as small as stars."

—from *Peter Pan*

With headphones snugly in place, Diamond glided down the mall, so intently focused on the music that she nearly crashed into a man heading in the opposite direction.

"Oh, I'm so sorry, sir. I wasn't paying attention," Diamond said, pulling out the buds.

"Not a problem, young lady. I'm just here to pick up

my daughter, and this place is a maze! Can you point me in the direction of the food court?"

Diamond laughed. "Turn around. It's right behind you."

The man, who looked to be about forty or so, was slender, handsome, and well dressed in a charcoal business suit. His dark blond hair, which looked to be spiked with just a touch of mousse, almost gleamed.

"Forgive my manners," the man said cordially. "I'm Thane English. My daughter is Chloe—maybe you know her? She a freshman at Broadway High School." He reached out his hand and shook Diamond's with a confident squeeze.

"I'm Diamond. I go to Broadway High too," Diamond said. "But I'm a sophomore. I don't know all the freshmen—it's a pretty big school."

"We just moved here a few weeks ago," the man told her. "Chloe's still adjusting; Broadway High is a lot different from the school she went to in California." He fell into step with her as they approached the sparsely populated food court. It smelled of cinnamon buns, strong coffee, and onions.

"I'd give anything to go to school in California," Diamond admitted as she bought two slices of cheese pizza.

"Why is that?" He glanced around, evidently looking for his daughter.

"I don't know. Close to Hollywood. Movie stars. The ocean. All that stuff," Diamond replied.

Thane tilted his head. "You have that look, if you don't mind my saying so."

"Huh? What look?"

He checked his watch. "Where can that girl be?" Then he looked back at Diamond as if he'd just remembered her question. "That star look. You're a dancer, right?"

Diamond's eyes went wide. "How did you know?"

"Well, you walk like a queen—tall and graceful. And it says 'dance' all over that bag you're carrying."

Diamond laughed. "Well, duh! Yeah, I've been dancing since I was four. My dream is to get on one of those shows like *So You Think You Can Dance* or *Dancing with the Stars*."

"You can do better than that," Thane replied. He looked around the food court once more. "She better not be late again," he grumbled.

"What do you mean?" Diamond sat down at a table and nibbled her pizza.

"Chloe is always late—drives me bonkers," he said, still glancing around.

"No, I mean, what did you mean when you said I could do better than being on a dance show?" Diamond asked.

"Well, my Chloe was in the last two Harry Potter movies and the first Twilight movie as well. Not huge parts, but she had small speaking roles in all of them."

Diamond almost choked on her food. "What? How?"

"I was the assistant director for all those films," Thane explained. "It helps. Chloe's got a portfolio that most kids her age would kill for. She's had a chance to work with some of the best teen actors."

"Wow. Lucky kid. So why did you move here to Nowheresville? There are no movie stars around here. Trust me. I would know."

"It's just temporary. We're filming a new movie here on location outside of town."

"Really? Why?"

His cell phone jingled. He pulled an iPhone from his pocket and glanced at the screen. "Excuse me, it's Chloe." He sat down at Diamond's table and slid the bar across the face of the phone. "Hey, sweetie. Where are you? I'm here at the mall, waiting for you in the food court, where you're supposed to be, talking to a classmate of yours from school." He stopped to laugh, giving his wedding ring a twirl. "Well, I'm glad you called, Chloe-girl. I'll see you at home. Tell Mom I already picked up the dog food." He tapped his phone off.

"She's already on her way home. Her mom and I got our wires crossed." He stood up and reached out his hand. "I gotta run. But it was a pleasure to meet you, Diamond."

"Me too," Diamond said, shaking his hand. She noticed his nails looked nicer than her own. Her pizza was growing cold.

Thane started to walk away from Diamond's table, then turned, frowned, and walked back. "I just had a thought," he said.

"A thought?"

"Would you like to meet Chloe and my wife and our goofy dog?"

Diamond tilted her head. "What?" She wasn't sure what he was asking.

"Chloe'd love to meet more kids from school, so I just thought you might . . . Well, of course you couldn't just

24

drop everything this minute . . ." Thane ran his fingers through his hair. "I just had a crazy idea—and Chloe's got some of her Hollywood friends visiting for the weekend. In fact"—he glanced at his watch—"their flight landed twenty-three minutes ago. But I'm sure it's too last-minute for you—forget I even mentioned it."

"Well, I'm waiting for someone, and I've got to get to dance. We have a performance tonight." But Diamond looked at him quizzically. Friends from Hollywood? She wondered what she might be passing up.

"Of course," Thane said. "I understand. You kids are always so busy. Chloe's friends are here to audition for the movie I mentioned. They know how to combine work and play!"

Diamond paused. Chloe's LA friends weren't just kids from California—they had to be actors and actresses! "You're casting this weekend?" she asked.

Thane shook his head. "I wish. I have to get my recommendations to the director tomorrow morning, so try-outs are tonight. It'll be tricky, because Diva Dawson and California Clover both want the main role, but I'm wanting a new face to grab that part."

"You're tellin' me Diva Dawson and California Clover are gonna be at your house?" Diamond was incredulous.

"Yep. A driver's at the airport right now."

This time it was Diamond who checked her watch. Practice started in half an hour, but she could be a little late. The show wasn't until seven thirty. And it was a chance to meet real movie stars! This was insane. "They're your daughter's *friends*?" she blurted out.

"Sure, since they were children. That's why Chloe was here at the mall—to get a new outfit for tonight. She goes crazy with my credit card!"

Diamond's heart began pounding. Could it be possible she had the chance to hang out with real movie stars?

"They're a great bunch of kids—they go to some pretty awesome parties together," Thane told Diamond with a smile. "But this is all so spur-of-the-moment—I just thought you'd like to meet them. But maybe next time."

Diamond hesitated. Would there ever *be* a next time? Stars like that in her hometown? "Wow. I'd give anything . . ."

Thane nodded. "It'd be pretty special—I can just imagine the photos you'd be able to post on Facebook."

"My friends will die of jealousy!" Diamond exclaimed. Then she glanced down at her flip-flops and cutoff tights and frowned. "I look like a mess. I'm dressed for dance, not for meeting famous people."

"Not a problem, great way to break the ice. Dancing, acting—it's all art." Then Thane thumped his forehead. "It just occurred to me—one of the key roles in the movie is a dance part! It's a modernization of *Peter Pan*."

"You're kidding!" Diamond jumped up from her seat. This was totally crazy! "Our studio is doing the ballet version of *Peter Pan* in June!"

It was Thane's turn to look surprised. "What a coincidence. I guess great ideas float in the universe at the same time." He paused. "So, what's your part? Wendy, I expect?"

Diamond flushed, embarrassed. "Uh, not exactly. I'm a pirate—Smee—and I'll probably fill in with a couple of small company parts."

"But not a lead?" Thane looked like he'd been personally insulted.

"Our teacher gives the big parts to different people every year. I'm hoping for the lead next year when we do *Cinderella*."

Thane frowned. "A year is a very long time to wait." He paused again. "Well, anyway, that settles that. I guess if you're already in a *Peter Pan*, you wouldn't be interested in our version."

"Sure I would! I'd love to see it when it comes out," Diamond told him as she picked the cheese off her pizza.

"I'll tell you what—why don't you aim for better than that? Why don't you try out for a role? You'd be just the kind of freshness I'm looking for in the part of Wendy."

"What? You're kidding." Diamond felt her heart racing. Was he for real?

"I never joke about my profession," Thane assured her. "In fact, I'd be honored if you'd try out for Wendy with the other kids."

"Me?" Flustered, Diamond didn't know what to say. "Now?" she managed.

"I know—it's pretty last-minute. But my director is antsy—we can't cast Pan until we cast Wendy, and I had to wait until some of the girls' schedules opened up— Ms. Dawson, for instance, is one busy lady! A half dozen other girls flew in from New York this morning from the Alvin Ailey studio—the part is an amazing opportunity for a dancer. But I have to be blunt—none of them have your presence."

Diamond tried to remember the last time someone told her she had "presence." Miss Ginger had often told her to stand straighter or balance better, but she'd never actually been given a compliment like that. "Really?" she sputtered.

Thane smiled. "I have no need to lie to you."

"But . . . but I can't leave my friend—she'll be here in a few minutes—and we have a show tonight," Diamond said, straining around to see if Mercedes was coming. Her mind was doing crazy spirals as she let herself think about the possibilities.

"I understand—really, I do. I wouldn't want you to miss your performance. "

"Actually, it's just a three-minute piece tonight called 'Pixie Dust.' Our teacher always does one group dance as a preview to our upcoming show—kinda like a teaser," Diamond explained.

"I can't believe how your universe seems to be colliding with ours," Thane said, shaking his head. "Do you at least have a good part in this one?"

Diamond frowned. "Nothing special. I'm in the back row."

"You feel like you ought to be in the front, don't you?" Thane asked.

Diamond nodded miserably. She hated to admit it, but he was right.

"Look, I know this is a little unusual, but leave your friend a note. Text her—whatever you kids do. Then as soon as we get to my house, we'll call your mother and have her come over to watch the auditions. She'll need to sign permission papers and income tax forms anyway."

"Permission? Tax forms? For what?"

"For you to audition. If you get the part, it would come with a significant salary." He paused and pursed his lips, as if he were thinking. "I'm not sure I could get you seven figures, as you're an unknown, but it would be at least half that."

"Half a million *dollars*?" Diamond reeled as she tried to visualize the number of zeros next to that dollar sign.

"That's the minimum going rate for a lead role in a movie. I'll be honest—kids already in the business make a lot more. But you've got to start somewhere." Thane nodded thoughtfully. "I've been in the business long enough to know when someone has that something special. And you, my dear, have that glow all over."

"I do?"

"You do."

"I couldn't possibly . . ."

Thane held both hands up. "I understand completely—I didn't mean to pressure. I wish we had another day, but as I said, the director wants to see first takes in the morning." He checked his watch.

Diamond's thoughts raced frantically. She imagined how proud her mom and Miss Ginger would be if she got a part in a real Hollywood movie. She thought back to the dozens of times her mother had told her to start thinking like a grown-up instead of a kid. Maybe it was time to start making her own decisions. This just seemed so right. But the show tonight . . .

To Thane she said, "This is a lot to think about. I'm really not sure what to do."

He looked her straight in he eyes. "Do what you know is right for *you*."

"I, uh . . ."

Thane offered his hand to Diamond once more. "It really was nice to meet you. Break a leg at your performance tonight; I know you'll be terrific. And I wish you luck in getting a better role in *Cinderella*. But I must hurry—I've got to go get the camera crew in place." He turned toward the exit.

It only took half a second. "Wait," Diamond called out. "Let me text my friend." She tapped the message in quickly, hoping her phone had enough juice to send it.

m,

ill call u ltr. i hve a chance 2 try out 4 the lead in a ptr pan dance movie w/ diva dawson and california clover. awesum, huh? my mom nos all abt it. (or she will soon.) sry 2 leave u out, but this was 2 good 2 pass up. tell miss g im sry 2 miss the sho, and not 2 b mad @ me. cyl

d

She sent the text, grabbed her hot pink dance bag, and left the mall with Thane English.

The rain continued. Thunder rumbled in the distance.

5

LAYLA, *Saturday, April 13   3:30 p.m.*

". . . a nameless fear clutched at her heart and made her cry."
—from *Peter Pan*

"She did *what?*" Zizi Cho cried out in disbelief, bugging her eyes out. Zizi was the studio comedy and drama queen. She could make herself hyperventilate over a lost peanut butter sandwich and distract an entire class into giggles as she mimicked Miss Ginger's moves behind her back.

But this was no time for humor. A half dozen dancers were huddled around Mercedes in the small rehearsal room behind the auditorium, which smelled of old sweat and fresh baby powder. Justin, hearing Zizi, hurried over and joined them.

Layla was staring at Mercedes, her hand over her mouth. "What's going on?" Justin asked.

"Diamond left the mall with somebody who told her she could be in a movie," Mercedes explained. "The *lead role*, she wrote in her text."

"How dumb is *that*?" Jillian Aylor said with a sniff, continuing her deep knee bends, exhaling breaths of superiority with each dip.

"She said in her text that California Clover and Diva Dawson are going to be in it," Mercedes added. "And it's gonna be based on *Peter Pan*, like our show."

"Shut *up*!" Zizi crossed her arms across her chest. "I'd *kill* to meet those two! And to be in a movie with them . . . man! It'll make our little performance look like a kindergarten show."

Jillian stood up straight and frowned. "If they've already cast two big stars for the movie, what do they need with Diamond? There's no way she'd get the lead part if they already have roles."

Mercedes cocked her head. "You know, you're right! I never looked at it that way. I guess Diamond didn't either."

"Did you tell Miss Ginger yet?" Zizi asked. Though she was shorter than the others, Zizi's prowess at unbelievably high leaps with seemingly little effort more than made up for her lack of height.

"Yeah, as soon as I got here. She was freakin' out, tryin' to locate Diamond's parents," Mercedes explained.

"Miss Ginger isn't canceling the show, is she?" Jillian asked as she held a stretch.

Mercedes and the others exchanged glances. That was just like Jillian—more interested in her own agenda than in anyone else.

"I don't think so," Mercedes said, "but I'm not sure if I can perform tonight. She took off with someone she didn't even *know*! I feel all messed up and kinda scared." Several other dancers nodded in agreement.

Layla told the group, "I heard Miss Ginger say the show will probably go on without Diamond, but I can't believe Diamond would dump us like this."

"Hang on a minute. If all this is on the level," Justin said, holding up his hands, "it's an amazing opportunity. Even if all she gets is a small role, that would be awesome."

"You really think she'll get a part?" Layla asked. She picked up a carrot stick from the fruit and veggie platter Miss Ginger always put out on performance nights—Layla worried about every pound she carried—and nibbled on it nervously. What she'd give to be as thin as Jillian!

Justin looked at Layla. "I bet if *you* took that carrot out of your mouth and auditioned, they'd give *you* the lead."

"Oooh, I heard that!" Zizi said. "You better not let Donovan hear you talkin' like that."

"I ain't sweatin' Donovan. I just gave my opinion," Justin said with a shrug.

Layla blushed and quickly turned to Mercedes. "So, do you think this is on the level?"

"I have no idea. All I know is what she texted me."

Mercedes fisted her hands to keep them from shaking. Then she admitted, "It seems pretty shady to me."

"Have you tried to call her?" Zizi asked.

"A million times—no answer. But her phone was almost out of juice when we were at the mall."

Layla pulled Mercedes into a hug and whispered miserably, "She's got no phone! How's she gonna get in touch with us?"

At that moment, Miss Ginger hurried into the rehearsal area. Her face was etched with worry. Diamond's parents were right behind her. Mrs. Landers looked stricken; her husband looked furious. He was clutching Shasta's hand tightly. Shasta looked like she was about to burst into tears.

"Mercedes, we need you a moment," Miss Ginger said, beckoning her over. Her friends moved closer so they could hear the conversation.

"Yes, Miss Ginger?"

Layla gasped as Miss Ginger said, "We've contacted the police, and they'll want to speak to you as soon as they get here."

"The police? Why? Diamond didn't do anything bad! Just stupid," Mercedes said, confusion on her face.

"Mercedes, she left the mall with a *stranger*—it's a potentially dangerous situation," Miss Ginger said, loud enough for them all to hear. "So we can't be too careful."

"Well, yeah, but . . ."

Diamond's mother reached out and touched Mercedes' hand. "Are you sure you didn't see who she left with? Do you know if it was a man or a woman?" she asked, desperation in her voice. "Why would she do something so foolish?"

Layla watched as Mercedes bit her lip and struggled with that impossible question. "No, I didn't see anybody. For real," Mercedes told them. "When I got to the food court, she was already gone. Like I told Miss Ginger, all I got was the text—the one I showed her."

"Diamond is pretty solid, Mrs. Landers," Justin added. "She wouldn't have gone with someone unless she felt pretty confident he was on the level."

"She'll call you in a minute, and you'll see—it's all a big freak-out over nothing," Layla chimed in.

"So why has no one heard from her?" Miss Ginger asked.

6

MERCEDES, *Saturday, April 13   4:30 p.m.*

"They sat thus night after night recalling that fatal Friday,
till every detail of it was stamped on their brains."
—from *Peter Pan*

Mercedes sat in an empty classroom, bouncing her leg
nervously. Steve sat with her, holding her hand.

"Hey, this is Mr. Baxson's classroom, right?"

Mercedes nodded and glanced around. Drawings
of the internal organs of frogs. Photos of endangered
reptiles and mammals. Animal cages. An acrid pet-shop
odor, almost masked by fresh cedar shavings. One small

hamster scampered feverishly in a wheel, the squeaky rhythm matching her heartbeat.

"I'm supposed to be getting ready for our show!" she said. "Why are they making me do this now?"

"At least they're not making you go down to the police station," Steve said, his voice calm.

"Yeah." Mercedes looked at him. "This is totally insane. I'm glad you're here—I'm scared."

Steve massaged her hand. "Everything is gonna be okay, babe. You'll see. Diamond'll call, everyone will yell at her, cops will come to school and give a don't-talk-to-strangers lecture, like in middle school, and life will go on."

"Are you sure?"

"I sure hope so."

"I just wish I had more to tell them, but I wasn't at the food court—I never saw anything," Mercedes said helplessly.

Steve stood up and peeked into the hall. "Uh-oh, here come some cops."

Moments later two police officers entered the room. Their clothes smelled damp, and their shoes left wet footprints on Mr. Baxson's floor.

Mercedes' parents followed behind them. She jumped up and ran to her mother, suddenly feeling like she might burst into tears. Her father touched her hair, patting it over and over.

"Please have a seat, folks," the taller of the two officers said.

Mercedes' dad just barely squeezed behind the classroom desk. She glanced over at him, and he patted his bulging belly and tried to make her smile. It didn't work. Her mother, still dressed in the suit she'd worn to work that morning, looked pale and worried.

"This won't take long. I'm Officer Lori Burrington, and this is my partner, Officer Jimmy Valido."

Valido was short and round, shaped like a jelly doughnut. Mercedes found herself wondering what would happen if he'd ever had to chase criminals like officers do on TV. Burrington was tall, muscular, and tough-looking, as if she'd been beating up on bad guys for a long time. Both of them wore black bulletproof vests that had POLICE in big white letters on the front and back.

"Why are you wearing bulletproof stuff?" Mercedes found the nerve to ask.

"Standard procedure these days. We wear them to go get ice cream," Valido told her.

"Please state your name and age." Officer Burrington's voice was no-nonsense.

"Mercedes Ford. I'm sixteen." Her voice sounded squeaky, and she cleared her throat.

"And you, sir?" Valido asked, turning to Steve.

"My name is Steven Wilkins. I'm seventeen; I'm her boyfriend."

"Were you with Diamond and Mercedes at the mall?"

"No, sir, I just heard about everything when I got here to see the show. I'm here for moral support, if that's all right."

Mercedes hoped they wouldn't make him leave, so she was relieved when they said nothing else to Steve. Burrington scribbled information in a notebook, while

Valido took notes on a small electronic tablet. He also snapped pictures of each of them, Mercedes blinking at the bright light from his camera.

"Can you tell us exactly what happened today at the mall, Mercedes?" asked Officer Burrington.

"There's really not much to tell," Mercedes said, feeling helpless. "We went to buy tights for tonight's show and get some pizza from the food court."

"The name of the store, please."

"C'est La Danse. It's our favorite dance store. But we didn't have time to fool around because we had to get here for our show."

"You and Diamond are both scheduled to be in tonight's performance?" Valido asked.

"Yes, sir."

"At some point the two of you separated?"

Mercedes lowered her eyes. "I, uh, bought a new leotard, and Diamond went on to the food court by herself. She was getting us both a slice. I'm so sorry!" She could not hold back the tears.

"This is not your fault," Burrington told her in a businesslike voice.

"You've gotta try not to blame yourself, sweetie," her mother added.

Fat chance, Mercedes thought.

"Do you have the receipt for the leotard?" Valido asked Mercedes.

"Uh—I guess so. Why?" Mercedes asked as she dug down into her dance bag and pulled out the purple one from the dance store. While searching for the receipt, she touched the silky fabric of the leotard—it made her skin crawl. She handed the whole bag to Officer Valido.

"Thank you. The time you bought the article is stamped on the receipt, and that will help us when we review security tapes at the mall."

"You haven't done that yet?" Mercedes asked. She looked from Steve to her parents in alarm.

"One thing at a time. We can do it much more quickly when we have an exact time to start from," Officer Burrington explained.

Mercedes glanced at her parents—they looked tense and nervous in the small school desks.

"Let's continue," Valido said, peering at the receipt. "So you separated shortly before 2:20 p.m. How much longer did you stay in the store?"

Mercedes tried to think. It was all such a blur. *Did I look at dance shoes? I think I glanced at Madame Jolie's new catalog while she was ringing me up. Did I go back and check out that new red warm-up? I think I did.* She felt nauseous.

She told the officers, "Maybe five minutes. No more than ten. Miss Ginger doesn't like for us to be late, so I hurried."

Officer Valido nodded. "And when you got to the food court, what did you do?"

"The food court is pretty small. I glanced around, but it was easy to see she wasn't there."

"So what did you do next?"

"I went to the ladies' bathroom to see if she'd had to make a pit stop. But all the stalls were open. I checked every single one."

The officers were taking notes furiously.

"Can you tell me what you did then?" Officer Burrington asked.

"I went back to the food court, and she still wasn't there. I thought maybe she'd decided to stop in one of the shops, so I tried to call her."

"And then?"

"When I opened my phone, I saw she had tried to call me. I think my phone must have been on vibrate, because I didn't hear it." Mercedes' mouth dropped open. "If I had answered when she called, she'd still be here, right?" Now new tears began to stream down her cheeks.

"No, dear," Officer Valido said. "You did everything right. Please go on."

Mercedes' mom hurried over and kneeled next to her. "Sh-sh. It's going to be okay. It's going to be okay."

Officer Barrington handed Mercedes a tissue. Then she asked, "When did you discover the text message?"

Mercedes looked up through her tears. "Right after I checked my voice messages. When I saw that text, I, like, panicked. It was so not like her—it was just plain crazy."

"Can you show it to me?" Officer Barrington asked.

Mercedes pulled her phone out of her purse, scrolled to the message, and, trembling, handed over the phone. Barrington studied it carefully while Officer Valido copied the message into his notebook.

"So you called your mother after you discovered the text message?" Valido asked.

"Well, first I called Diamond's cell, like, a million times, but it just went to voice mail—she'd told me in the car that her phone was out of juice. Then I called my mother. And she called Diamond's mom. I guess Diamond's mom called you."

Officer Valido stood and stretched. "You've been very helpful, Mercedes. I know this has been difficult, but your information will really help us to start the search for Diamond."

Officer Barrington shook her hand. "We may have follow-up questions. We'll be in touch. I hope you have a great performance tonight."

"Not likely," Mercedes said with a sigh.

"May we keep this leotard and receipt for a few days?" Valido asked.

"Keep it forever," Mercedes replied. "I will never, ever wear that thing!"

7

DIAMOND, *Saturday, April 13   2:45 p.m.*

"Take care, lest an adventure is now offered you,
which, if accepted, will plunge you into deepest woe."
—from *Peter Pan*

The ride from the mall to Thane's house took only about ten minutes. The rain continued; the day looked like a thick gray wool blanket.

Diamond, more nervous about meeting movie stars than riding in a car with a complete stranger, breathed deeply. The seats were real leather, and new! She stifled a giggle when she thought about telling Mercedes she'd actually ridden in a Mercedes!

"Want to see a picture of Chloe? I've got some on my phone," Thane said as they paused at red light. He pulled up a photo on his iPhone and handed it to Diamond.

She gazed at the attractive wife, the ruddy Irish setter, and a teenager who must be Chloe—she was pencil thin and blond.

"There are more—you're welcome to scroll across," he said, so she did, seeing several fuzzy photos of Chloe with movie stars and singers that Diamond had only seen in magazines.

"Your daughter sure is lucky," Diamond said.

"Yes, she's a good kid. She doesn't even know how charmed her life is. I guess she thinks everybody grows up on a movie set."

"I'm a little nervous," Diamond admitted. "I've only auditioned for parts in school plays and dance recitals."

"An audition is an audition! So relax and be yourself. You'll do fine."

The rain beat down upon the car. Diamond watched the droplets zigzag down the side of the window. She thought with a pang about the performance she was missing; without thinking, she scraped the polish off three of her fingernails.

"We're almost there," Thane said, as if reading her mind.

Diamond reached into her pocket for her phone. "I better call my mom. She's gonna kill me for ditching this performance. She pays a lot of money for my classes."

"Great idea," Thane replied. "I'll give you the address so you can tell her where to meet you."

Diamond fumbled in her pockets and took her phone

out. It was then that she discovered that the battery was completely dead.

"Aw, man—I'm out of juice," Diamond cried out. "And I left my charger at home."

"Not to worry. You can use my phone—oh wait, we're here! You can call her as soon as we get in the house." Thane pulled into a long driveway lined with thick shrubbery, which snaked through increasingly dense trees. It seemed they drove for almost half a mile before the road cleared and they finally drew up in front of a huge stone home. A rainbow of spring flowers—tulips, hyacinths, and daffodils—were in full bloom in what looked to be a professionally groomed garden in the front of the house. It was like something straight out of a magazine.

A sleek red Irish setter bounded toward the car, coat dripping and feet muddy. Diamond relaxed a bit.

"Whoa, Bella!" Thane said, swinging open his door. "Did Chloe leave you out in the rain? Poor baby! I'll clean you up in a minute."

"Nice house. It looks like a museum! Makes mine look like a barn," Diamond said as she got out of the car. The manicured shrubs and perfectly placed flowers seemed to shimmer in the rainwater, and stone walkways made the place perfect.

Thane laughed and petted the wet dog's head. "Meet Bella. After filming all those *Twilight* flicks, what other name could we give her?"

"Where are, uh, the others?" Diamond asked. She didn't see any other cars in the huge, circular driveway.

"Probably still collecting luggage." He laughed.

"California doesn't get the idea of a 'weekend bag'— probably they had to hire a second car just for her luggage." He looked at Diamond and added wryly, "When you get to be a big star, promise me you'll get to shoots on time."

Diamond managed a grin and hurried with him to the huge, carved front door, hoping the rain wouldn't mess up her hair. The dog trotted away after a squirrel.

Thane punched in a key code, listened for the tone, then opened the door. She wasn't sure, but it looked like mahogany. Thane ushered her inside with a "Welcome!" As he closed the door, he re-set the alarm.

"Won't the others need to get in?"

"I can't be too cautious. We don't want paparazzi snooping. The driver will ring when he gets here with California and Diva."

"How would the paparazzi know?" Diamond asked.

"Oh, those girls, they hate attention, they love attention. One of them will make sure someone on the plane knows who they are, and soon texts and tweets—'You won't believe who was on the plane with me!'—start to fly. Bingo—word's out."

Diamond nodded. *Boy, it's a whole different world,* she thought. She looked around—the living room was also a whole different world, spacious and lovely. One entire wall was a sort of fountain, water flowing from ceiling to floor. Soft lighting made the leather furniture look inviting and comfortable. What looked to be movie scripts were stacked on a huge table.

"This is really nice," Diamond said, running her hand

along the table's polished wood. It was silky smooth. "Where's Chloe?" She could hardly wait to meet her and her movie star friends. She couldn't believe she was just minutes away from meeting California Clover and Diva Dawson.

"Good question! Chloe!" Thane called. "Are you here, honey? Daddy's home. I want you to meet someone. Alexandria? Where are you two?"

Diamond picked up one of the scripts—it was labeled *Neverland Dancer.* She smiled, then gasped as she saw the title of the script below it. "*A Screenplay for Harry Potter and the Sorcerer's Stone,*" she whispered in amazement. She carefully thumbed through the well-worn, highlighted, and underlined scripts. "Wow." One was signed by Daniel Radcliffe. "Is this really the signature of the guy who played Harry Potter?" Diamond asked with astonishment.

"Sure. Dan's a good friend."

Impressed, Diamond sat down on the edge of one of the couches and began to read. She'd never read a real screenplay before, but she'd seen all the movies. It was cool to see the character's words printed out—words she'd heard half a dozen times watching reruns of those films.

Thane's phone rang again. "Alexandria! Where are you? What do you mean, new shoes? She has a hundred pairs of shoes. Okay. Okay. But I brought a friend for her to meet—a girl from the high school—she'll be auditioning tonight. So be quick. Love you. Bye."

"Shoes?" Diamond said, looking up.

"They'll be here in ten minutes, promise. I'm sorry about the confusion. Welcome to my family on audition day. Would you like a Coke or a glass of water?"

"Yes, please, a Diet Coke. And, uh, can I use your phone to call my mom? She needs to know where I am."

"Absolutely. Let me just get you that cola first."

Thane went over to a bar area, opened a small refrigerator, and pulled out a bottle. He twisted the cap off, adding ice to a glass before pouring the soda. It was still fizzing when he brought it to her.

Diamond gulped it down. Pizza made her so thirsty!

Thane offered to refill it, but Diamond shook her head. He took the empty glass from her and said, "Chloe is on her way, and then the auditions for *Neverland Dancer* can begin." For some reason his voice was sounding strangely gummy—as if he were speaking though syrup.

Diamond giggled at the thought of maple-covered lips and hands. Then she laughed out loud as she imagined the scene from the Disney version of *Peter Pan*, where seemingly perfectly normal children went flying out of their bedroom window. Willingly. With a stranger. *What's up with that?* She tried to wrap her thoughts around the idea, but her brain felt like melting marshmallows.

"I need to call my moom, my moon, I mean my muvver," she said. Her mouth—wasn't mouthing. Ha! She shook her head, which oddly felt like it was unattached to her body—a balloon afloat in soda bubbles. She dropped the script she'd been looking at.

Thane walked over slowly and picked it up. "Are you okay, Diamond?"

"What's happing, happing, hapning to me?" she said, trying to keep her voice from slurring.

Thane picked up his phone and snapped it open. "She's ready," it seemed like he said.

Diamond leaned back on the sofa, her head spinning, the world spinning. She closed her eyes.

8

"'So, Pan,' said Hook at last, 'this is all your doing.'
"'Ay, James Hook,' came the stern answer, 'it is all my doing.'"
—from *Peter Pan*

Layla sat on the floor in costume and makeup, waiting for the others for the pre-performance activities that Miss Ginger insisted on. First practice. Then pep talk and prayer.

Mercedes slipped into the tiny room and sat beside her, stretching a little.

"You okay?" Layla asked.

"Talking to the cops freaked me out," Mercedes confessed. "How am I supposed to dance after that?"

Layla met her eyes. "I don't know if Diamond is kidnapped or at a party with movie stars. But somehow I'm not feeling a party." She spritzed more hair spray on her wayward curls.

"Yeah, me neither," Mercedes admitted. "I got this bad feeling. Damn it! I never should have let her go to the food court alone."

"Hey, you can't swallow this blame," Layla told her. "That mall is like our second home. There was no way you could have guessed something bad would happen."

"Yeah, I know, but I still feel responsible. I didn't need that new leotard! We shoulda stayed together. If I had just . . ."

Trying to distract her, Layla asked, "Did Steve bring your candy?"

Mercedes looked up and gave a small smile. "Yeah. He's my sweet-talkin', sugar-coated candy man," she said, humming an old Christina Aguilera song. "He brings me candy to every show."

"'Candyman' is one of Diamond's favorites," Layla mused, smoothing the lines of her costume. "Her mom must be losing it. Diamond is *so* gonna be on punishment—probably till she dies!"

Mercedes sucked in her breath. "Don't say that word, girl!" She retightened the ribbons on her pointe shoes. "I'm sorry—I'm being crazy. Is your mom coming tonight?"

"I hope so. Sometimes she has to do double shifts at

the diner. It's all right if she misses this one." Layla said it breezily, but a tinge of sadness edged her voice. "She's got my back most of the time."

"Yeah, that's usually my dad, too. He rolls up ten seconds before the curtain rises, pulling up late in his big, loud diesel truck. I think he loves that truck more than me!"

"Not a chance. I've seen how your father looks when you're dancing, Mercedes. Like you're some kind of magical Disney princess," Layla said, unable to keep a touch of envy from her voice.

"Hah! I hope not. Those Disney girls have, like, ten-inch waistlines. How do they breathe?" Mercedes asked.

"They're cartoons!"

"Duh."

Both girls laughed, then Layla said softly, "I wish *my* dad could see me dance."

"How long has it been?" Mercedes asked carefully.

"Six years now. He got sent away when I was ten. I should be used to him being gone, but it still sucks."

"Does dancing help?" Mercedes asked.

"It totally saved me. It was my dad who found Miss Ginger's when I was in first grade; he's the one who convinced my mom to let me try out the classes. It's like somehow he knew that dancing made me feel real."

"Deep."

"He used to wait in the parking lot every night until I finished class."

"I remember! Sometimes you guys would give me a ride home. Didn't he always have a strawberry smoothie waiting in the cup holder for you?"

"Yep." Layla tried to smile, remembering. "He never missed a pickup. He never missed a show. And then he was gone."

"Do you want to talk about it?" Mercedes asked. Other dancers were beginning to trickle in, stretching, talking quietly, preparing mentally.

"Not really. We've got enough drama going on tonight."

"True that," Mercedes agreed.

Still, as she stretched, Layla found herself thinking more about her dad. She had never found out all the exact details, but somehow her father had ended up being the driver while two of his friends robbed a con-venience store—and one of them was armed. He swore he didn't know what they had planned to do, but the jury didn't believe him, and he'd been plucked from her life.

Mercedes, noting her friend's sad face, slung her arm across her shoulders. "Dance tonight for your daddy," she whispered.

"Thanks, girl," Layla told Mercedes. "I got this now. Let's do it."

9

MERCEDES, *Saturday, April 13   6 p.m.*

"'She thinks we have lost the way' . . . 'and she is rather frightened.'"
—from *Peter Pan*

Miss Ginger clapped her hands together to get everyone's attention. "Circle up, guys. It's almost time." She sat down on the floor between Zizi and Jillian. Justin, Mercedes noticed, had positioned himself between Layla and Jillian. Almost twenty-five young dancers between the ages of fourteen and seventeen joined the circle.

"I can't find the sash to my costume, Miss Ginger," Tara Picassa whined.

Her twin sister, Tina, said, "You're sitting on it, silly." The fourteen-year-olds were the youngest performers in the spring showcase, and they seemed to wear their nerves on their slender shoulders.

"OMG! What if I forget my dance?" Zizi cried out.

Mercedes shook her head. Who but Zizi would actually talk in text? She wasn't sure if Zizi was exaggerating like she usually did or if the stress was really getting to her.

"You won't, Zizi. Just relax, all of you," Miss Ginger said in what the girls called her calming voice. "Breathe deeply. Silence. Breathe again."

"Have you heard anything more about Diamond?" Elizabeth Flemming asked.

"No, Lil Bit. I haven't. But I have faith in my prayers."

Although she was fifteen, Elizabeth was pixie-tiny and looked like she was eleven or twelve. She couldn't have weighed more than eighty-five pounds. Everybody, including her teachers, called her Lil Bit.

She's perfect for the part of Tinker Bell, Mercedes thought appraisingly.

"I feel all messed up inside," Layla admitted to the group. Everyone seemed to nod in agreement.

"Maybe we should cancel the show," Lil Bit suggested quietly. "It doesn't seem right somehow."

Miss Ginger looked carefully at the dancers circled around her. "I'm listening. Does anyone feel strongly about not dancing tonight?"

The group was silent for a moment, then Justin spoke up. "We're all sorta nervous, but we really don't know anything bad has happened."

"Diamond might even show up in a few minutes, making crazy excuses about being late," Zizi suggested.

"Or maybe she won't," Layla added ominously.

"Stop that!" Mercedes cried out. "We need to dance because Diamond would expect us to!"

"Are we all agreed?" Miss Ginger asked.

A quiet chorus of yeses responded.

"We're going to include Diamond in our prayer," Miss Ginger said. "Praying is all I've been doing since I heard about her disappearance."

"Do you think it will be on the *news*?" Zizi said dramatically. "I've never known anybody from an Amber Alert before. I think it would be cool to have your name used in an official police capacity."

"Chill, Zizi. The child who had Amber Alert named after her did not survive," Miss Ginger explained, her tone serious.

"Oh." Zizi looked stricken. "I didn't know. Sorry."

"I'm not sure if they will post an Amber Alert. There's so much we just don't know at this point," Miss Ginger told them.

Mercedes wrapped her arms around her head and squeezed. This was *so* hard!

"This is *not on you*," Layla whispered. "No blame—got it?"

Mercedes nodded and tried to relax. She could feel the love and concern Miss Ginger's eyes reflected as she looked at them all. She paused before she spoke. "This show is a little different tonight, my young friends, because one of our own is missing, and we're all worried. But for the few minutes each of you are onstage, I want you to concentrate on your dance, on your skill, on your God-given talent."

"I'm scared I'll mess up, like I can't find my zone," Lil Bit admitted.

"You won't. All your hard work and practice comes down to this moment in time, and I don't want any of you to stress tonight. Have *fun*. Diamond is right here with us. And Zizi, you forgot to put on your lipstick."

Zizi shrieked and slapped her hands to her mouth. "Oops! My bad. I'll be sure to do it before the curtains open. Or I can do my makeup onstage, just to stall for time. The audience might like to see me do a lipstick dance."

"Enough, Zizi!" Miss Ginger said. "I'm not in the mood for your silliness tonight."

Zizi tried to explain. "I'm just trying to lighten things up. Everybody is about to crash and cry."

"She's kinda right," Layla admitted.

"I'm still worried about the 'Pixie Dust' preview dance, Miss Ginger," Mercedes admitted. "It's gonna look funny without Diamond."

"Look. It's just like if somebody is sick and misses a rehearsal class. Don't we just fill in that space?"

"But if we fill in Diamond's place tonight, won't it seem like we don't care?" Mercedes' voice caught, and the tears came.

Jillian reached over and handed Mercedes a tissue. "Fix your face, girl. Diamond is expecting you to dance like a Broadway star tonight!"

Mercedes sniffed and wiped her eyes carefully. "Thanks, Jillian. And hey . . ."

"Yeah?

"You're not the icebox I thought you were."

"Me? Cold?" Jillian shrugged the idea away.

Miss Ginger glanced at her circle of young people and said, "Join hands, dancers. Feel the strength of each other. I'm going to start by squeezing Zizi's hand. Then I want you each to squeeze the hand of the person next to you until I feel that power return to my hand." She began.

When Mercedes felt a strong, assured squeeze from Tina, she felt a little of the power going around the circle, then she quickly passed it to Layla.

A few moments later, Miss Ginger said, "I'm very proud of each and every one of you," she said. "You are each unique and so very special to me and to the Crystal Pointe Dance Academy. We are all very blessed."

"Is this when we do the prayer?" Lil Bit asked in a whisper.

"Yes, Lil Bit, I think it's the perfect time for a little help from above," Miss Ginger replied. "First, let's say a special word for Diamond. Lord, please be with Diamond tonight, and please let her find her way back home safely."

"Amen," the group said.

"Now, let's say our group prayer together."

They all bowed their heads and, still holding hands tightly, they said in unison, "Lord, bless this stage as we dance tonight, bless the dancer to my left and right. Bless my head down to my toes, and if I mess up, I pray no one knows. Thank You for the music, thank You for the lights, thank You for the gift of DANCE that we will share tonight. Amen."

Miss Ginger beamed. "What's the point?" she asked them. They all knew the chant.

"Crystal Pointe!"

"What's the point?"

"Crystal Pointe!"

"What's the point?"

"Crystal Pointe! Yay, Crystal Pointe Studio!"

Feeling newly energized and now less shaky from the police interview, Mercedes joined the others as they moved to their places for the curtains to open.

She hated that Diamond was missing this—the traditions, the repetitions, the drama of pre-show preparations. She hoped Diamond was having fun.

10

DIAMOND, *Saturday, April 13   7:30 p.m.*

"If you shut your eyes and are a lucky one, you may see at times a shapeless pool of lovely pale colours suspended in the darkness."
—from *Peter Pan*

Diamond awoke to darkness. She felt oddly woozy, and even though she kept blinking, she couldn't see a thing. When she turned her head even slightly, a pounding headache made her close her eyes once more.

Where am I? she thought groggily. Then she remembered Thane and the dog named Bella and the daughter she never got to meet. *Did I miss the auditions?* She tried to remember, but her head felt like clotted cream. She waited a few minutes, then took a deep breath and tried to sit up. But her body seemed to be glued. To what? She couldn't move!

Her arms—*Oh God,* they were tied, stretched above her head. She seemed to be lying on something soft—a bed? And she was freezing. Why was she so cold? Then, with a lurch of horror, she realized that she was wearing only her underwear. Where were her clothes? *Oh my God! Oh my God!* Where were her clothes?

Diamond tried to move once more, but her arms were held immobile. *Ropes?* she wondered, confused, shaky. *Ropes? What's going on?*

She went deadly still. Rain pounded outside a window, thunder rumbled in the distance. A flash of lightning illuminated the room for just a second. She could make out furniture—a chest of drawers, a chair. Two bulky square-shaped objects against a wall. She noticed a door to her left. *But where were her clothes?*

She pulled and tugged, but there was no slack in the ropes; she could not pull her arms free. She panicked.

That's when she began to scream.

11

"He had had ecstasies innumerable that other children can never know;
but he was looking through the window at the one joy from
which he must be for ever barred."
—from *Peter Pan*

Justin liked to prepare himself mentally and physically for
a performance. He always found a place in the very back
of the wings of the stage where he could stretch comfort-
ably and think through his pieces. He had a break-dance
solo, as well as a ballet pas de deux with Jillian. His dad was
videotaping both pieces—they could be used for college

auditions if he did well. He was worried about Diamond, but right now all he could do was focus on the show.

He figured out long ago that on show days a lot of girls tended to be twittery and nervous, so he'd learned to stay out of their way. But he always positioned himself so he could see and hear everything that was going on, especially when Layla was about to perform—he couldn't help himself.

"You ready?" he heard Zizi whisper to Layla as the two stood in the wings behind the first curtain. Zizi, he knew, was probably doing something silly and distracting, like telling jokes to make Layla laugh.

"Been ready," Justin heard Layla reply. "I can do these steps in my sleep, girl, 'cause I'm always scared I'll mess up."

"Your piece is complicated," Zizi continued. "Don't be trippin' out there! And I mean it both ways." She made a silly face, then fell to the floor in a heap, like a rag doll.

"Girl, you crazy! Get up before you get your costume dirty." Layla reached down and pulled Zizi to her feet. "Miss Ginger would have a fit if she saw you." She brushed specks off Zizi's costume, a pale aquamarine leotard with a thin, silky skirt, studded with sequins that shimmered under stage lights.

Layla wore an all white, sequin-studded piece of froth that glistened against her copper-colored skin. Zizi looked cute, Justin thought, but Layla was stunning.

And dudes laugh at me! I'm in heaven! Justin thought with a wry smile.

Jillian was onstage, finishing her solo. Justin peeked from backstage and nodded approvingly as she did a triple pirouette, her pointe shoes barely making a sound as she spun effortlessly with the music.

The final strains of the music, as bold and strong as Jillian's leaps, echoed in the background. The cheers and applause from the audience resounded. Jillian took her bows gracefully, then trotted off the stage in that awkward walk of girls who would prefer to be on pointe, in the air, above the rest of the world, rather than walking flat-footed on solid ground in heavy-toed pointe shoes.

Her makeup smeared with sweat, Jillian pushed Zizi and Layla out of her way, headed to the nearest garbage can, and threw up. Jillian always vomited after her performances. As Zizi said, she danced like the devil, then she puked.

Tara and Tina were on next, doing a duet to "Almost There" from the movie *The Princess and the Frog*. They almost knocked Justin over as they scurried onstage.

"Hey, good job," Justin told Jillian as she straightened up from the wastebasket and joined him at the curtain. "You nailed it."

Jillian simply nodded and waved her water bottle in acknowledgment. She wouldn't talk to anyone for the next ten minutes or so. It was just her routine. Still, Zizi rolled her eyes and mouthed *lah-dee-dah* to Layla.

"We all got issues," Layla said with a shrug. She leaned over and touched her toes, then placed the flat of her hands on the floor. Justin was in awe of her flexibility. He'd watched her during rehearsals; even dressed in sweaty practice clothes, she always looked like she was floating, swimming, gliding. . . .

"What are *you* doing backstage?" Zizi cried out suddenly. "You're gonna get us all busted, dude!"

Justin was so busy thinking about Layla that at first he thought Zizi was talking to *him*. But when he saw where she was looking, he frowned.

Layla pulled up from her stretch and gasped. Standing before her was Donovan.

"Donny, why are you here?" Layla whispered frantically. "I go on next!"

"I know." He crossed his arms, his finely chiseled face hard and unsmiling.

"Why aren't you in the audience?" Layla asked, her eyes flitting back and forth, probably looking out for Miss Ginger.

"I just wanted to wish you good luck in person," Donovan said, taking her arm. But his voice sounded more threatening than encouraging, it seemed to Justin.

"Uh, thanks, but I need to focus right now." She tried to ease away from him.

"Sure you do." He grinned coldly. "On me." He pushed his body closer to hers. Layla stepped back, bumping into the wall.

"Leave her alone!" Justin finally said.

"This ain't got nothin' to do with you, man," Donovan snarled. "Back off."

Justin crossed his arms; his biceps went taut. "No. *You* back off. Layla has to dance next, and she needs to concentrate. Now LEAVE HER ALONE!"

Donovan swung around to face Justin, fire in his eyes.

Layla stepped between them. "I got this, Justin." She

was paler than Justin had ever seen her. She took Donovan by the arm, moved him one step away from Justin, then stroked his face. She said calmly, "First the dance. Then you."

Donovan looked her up and down. "What's that you wearin'?"

"It's my costume!" she answered, frustration in her voice. But Justin noticed she pulled the edge of her leotard farther down over her butt cheeks. "You shouldn't be backstage, Donny. You'll get me in trouble."

"I don't like it," he snarled. "All I can see is your boobs and your butt."

"I'm a dancer," she replied angrily. "It's what we wear. Now go sit down in the audience!"

"That's my beef," he continued, still in her space. "You *show* too much. And you look to me like you're gaining weight!"

Layla paused. "I do?" She looked down at her thighs.

"Who you showin' off for?" Donny hissed.

"Please," she said, lowering her voice. "Let's talk about this after the performance."

"Change your clothes!" he demanded.

"You're crazy! I'm up next." She reached out to him, pleading.

He grabbed both her wrists, hard. "No girl of mine is gonna dance like a stripper!"

In tears now, Layla pushed him away. "It's *ballet*!"

Justin's hands curled into fists. It took all his control not to lash out.

The music from the twins' dance trumpeted cheerfully.

66

Justin was vaguely aware of cheers from the audience. The twins were probably doing the acrobatic part of their routine.

Donovan grabbed Layla's arm and squeezed. "I'm always first. Remember that."

Justin unfisted and refisted his hands. He'd noticed bruises on Layla's wrists a few times, and sometimes her face looked oddly swollen. But girls wore makeup, and he couldn't be sure what he was seeing. He'd never said anything before, but man, he was about bust on that punk. He was just *standing* there, letting Donovan manhandle Layla. He should have clocked him! He wanted to comfort Layla—someone had to tell her she didn't have to put up with that kind of stuff.

"Always, Donny," Layla was saying.

Donovan then pulled her face close to his, kissed her roughly, and exited just as Miss Ginger hurried toward them, glaring.

"No boyfriends backstage, Layla! You know that! Shoo, you!" she said to Donovan.

"I'm sorry, Miss Ginger. I had no idea he'd show up like that," Layla was saying shakily. "It won't happen again." She rubbed her arm and hurriedly wiped the tears from her face.

Justin hovered, taut and tense.

Donovan eased away like oil.

12

JUSTIN, *Saturday, April 13   7:45 p.m.*

"Oh, the cleverness of me!"
—from *Peter Pan*

The stage was black. Justin was dressed all in white—his shoes, loose pants, and unbuttoned, long-sleeved, silky shirt would almost glow in the spotlight. He wore a white baseball cap, brim turned to the back, that fit snugly over his braids. He liked to keep his hair long so it could move with him.

He blinked when the focused beam of the spotlight shone directly on him, making it impossible for him to see beyond the edge of the stage. It didn't matter anyway, because he was about to be fused with the beat. He was about to be movement and rhythm. He was about to be sound in motion.

The audience waited. He could feel their anticipation. He was on it. Putting everything else—Layla, Donovan, anger—behind him, he inhaled, drawing air all the way down to his stomach. A brief nod cued his music—"Boom Boom Pow" by The Black Eyed Peas. He began.

He started with a toprock, gentle pops of his arms and upper body while his feet became the snare of the drum. Slowly gaining momentum and speed, but exercising absolute control, he transitioned to a floor rock, twisting his lower body and moving his feet so swiftly they seemed to be liquid. His entire body became his instrument.

Even though he'd practiced this piece dozens of times, he never danced it the same way twice. Each time he let his imagination guide him. He transitioned to a helicopter, his feet swinging around in a continuous motion. He bounced up. He rolled over. His limbs moved so fast, it seemed they would tangle.

He performed a series of freezes where he suspended himself off the ground using only the strength of his upper body. After several backflips, he moved to a flare, his hands on the floor now, his body twirling above him as his hands became his feet. The audience roared with approval.

In a swift kinetic transition, he moved to a windmill, a swipe, then smoothly to a hurricane, a head spin done with both arms around his head.

As the music pounded—*boom boom pow*—Justin's whole being kept up with it. He bounced back up and ended with a difficult power move in which he spun around in a circular motion, almost like a skater on ice, but he had only the swiftness of his feet to propel him. As the music throbbed to its conclusion, Justin doffed his hat to the audience and took a deep bow to cheers and yells and hoots of appreciation.

He stayed a moment longer than he probably should have, but the enthusiasm of the crowd felt *so* good. He owned that stage.

13

LAYLA, *Saturday, April 13   9:30 p.m.*

"'Why can't you fly now, mother?'

"'Because I am grown up, dearest. When people grow up they forget the way.'"

—from *Peter Pan*

"We're not goin' out to eat, are we?" Zizi asked Layla, who had changed into sweats like most of the other dancers had after the recital. Several of the girls had gathered in the lobby. Layla peeked outside the huge metal doors of the school auditorium. It was still pouring out. Donovan's Escalade stood waiting, idling right in front, probably with the music blasting.

Audience members milled around the lobby as well, waiting for their dancers to come from backstage. Parents snapped photos, and most girls posed with bouquets of flowers—the traditional gift for after a show. But Layla had a headache and just wanted to get out of there.

"No, girl. Not after I messed up like I did," Layla told Zizi. "I just want to go home and sleep." She still couldn't believe what a disaster her performance had been: She had missed a turn, slipped, and fallen. Even though she'd recovered quickly and continued the dance perfectly, she knew she had disappointed Miss Ginger. She'd sure disappointed herself. She'd never fallen during a performance before! She glanced out the door again to where Donovan waited in his car. She knew he wanted her to hurry.

"How can you guys even think about food?" Mercedes asked, coming up behind them with Steve. "Aren't you worried about Diamond?"

"No word?" Jillian asked. "I figured she was home with her mom by now."

"No. Her cell phone's gotta be out of juice. Otherwise she woulda texted me by now, telling me all about what was going on. You don't hang out with movie stars and not text it and tweet it to everybody you know!"

"True that," Layla said. "Hey! Don't they have surveillance video of the doors to malls? Wouldn't they have this guy on tape?"

"Yeah, the cops are looking, but I don't think it's like on TV, where they get those tapes before the first commercial," Mercedes explained. "It takes a long time for stuff to happen in the real world. But they're check—" She was interrupted by the loud, long honk of a car horn.

Layla almost jumped. "Donovan," she said with a sigh. "Time to go. He's gotta go to work after he takes me home."

"Girl, that dude sure has got you on a tight chain," Jillian remarked.

"You don't know what you're talking about. Donovan is the best thing that ever happened to me," Layla shot back.

"You bombed your dance because of him," Jillian said, exasperated. "He made you lose your concentration, showing up backstage."

"That was *not* Donny's bad," Layla replied hotly. "I was the only one on that stage. I just messed up."

Jillian touched Layla's arm. "Whatever! I gotta go. See you at the studio next week." She waved at her mother, who was pointing to the red roses she always brought for her. The two of them left together, arm in arm.

Zizi's parents walked up next. "Great job tonight, ladies," Zizi's dad told them. Zizi did an elaborate jeté, bowed deeply, and kissed her parents on both cheeks. "*Merci,* my *maman et papa,*" she said in a fake French accent.

Her parents shook their heads, laughing. With a grand sweep of her arms, Zizi's mom said to the cluster of dancers, "Superb as always."

"Thanks, Mr. and Mrs. Cho," Layla replied for them all. She tried not to think about the way Zizi's dad looked at Zizi like she was on the red carpet for the Academy Awards, even when she acted like a nutcase. She wondered what her own dad was doing at this moment.

"Did you hear about Diamond Landers, Dad?" Zizi asked, her voice an exaggerated whisper.

"No, what happened?"

"We're not sure. But she might have been kidnapped by someone from the mall. Maybe a gang!"

Layla frowned. "We don't *know* that yet, Zizi, and it was probably just one person."

Zizi's mom, with shock in her voice, asked, "But how could that happen? Didn't anybody try to stop him? I don't understand!"

Zizi grasped her parents' hands. "From what we know, she went with this dude willingly."

"She what?" Zizi's father looked at his wife, then back to Zizi. "You wouldn't do anything like that, would you?" her dad asked.

"Not if I thought about it first, Daddy. But you know me—duh!" Zizi shrugged. Then she added, "Whoever it was must have been awfully convincing. Or really cute." She paused, and then said with absolute seriousness, "It's really scary, Dad." And she turned from her friends to bury her face against her father's chest.

"Her parents must be crazy with worry!" Mrs. Cho exclaimed.

"We all are," Mercedes replied, glancing over to Steve. Layla noticed Steve speaking quietly to Mercedes' mom, who actually hugged him. She couldn't imagine Donny and her mother even shaking hands.

"I'll call or text you later," Zizi said to Layla. "Let me know the minute you hear anything about Diamond, okay?"

"Gotcha."

Just then Layla saw her own mom hurrying over. She carried no bouquet. She looked tired and smelled of fried chicken. But Layla was happy to be drawn into her embrace. "Glad you came, Mom."

"I'm sorry, honey," she said. "Cook wouldn't let me go—we had a busload of teenagers stop in."

Layla made a face. "Oh, that's the worst!"

"Loud, rude, and hungry—fifty of them!"

"I'm sorry you had put up with that, Mom. But you didn't miss anything."

"But I did! Your solo! I felt so bad."

"I didn't do so good tonight anyway," Layla admitted.

"Nonsense. You're always amazing, even when you think you mess up."

"I *fell*, Mom."

Her mother's eyes grew wide. "Oh, no! Did you hurt yourself?"

"No, just my pride. I made an ass of myself. And I *knew* that dance, inside and out." Layla sighed. "Mom, can we maybe talk about some stuff tonight? I'll send Donny on his way, and I can ride with you."

"Tonight? Oh, sweetie, can we talk about it in the morning? You'll see things differently then anyway." Layla's mother dug in her purse and pulled out her cell phone.

Layla's heart sank. "Are you going out?" she asked, even though she knew the answer.

"I've got a date," her mom said, a distracted smile lighting her face as she scrolled through her text messages.

A too-familiar pressure tightened in Layla's chest. She lowered her voice and said angrily, "You and Daddy are *not* divorced! He's coming *back*!" She and her mother had had this conversation far too many times.

"Layla, I'm not going to marry the guy—we've been over this! I just deserve a little fun in my life," her mother replied in exasperation.

"Well, I hope you take a shower before you go out," Layla lashed back. "You stink of chicken grease!"

"And I bothered to hurry over and see you!" Mrs. Ridgewood fumed. "Tell Donovan to have you home at a decent hour."

Her eyes stinging with tears, Layla looked around and hoped no one had heard their conversation. The lobby was almost empty. Justin was leaning against a table, waiting for his dad, but he wasn't looking her way.

Layla's mother hurried out without saying good-bye. *How did that go downhill so fast?* Layla wondered dejectedly. As she headed toward Donovan's car, Layla thought about Diamond and the devastation her parents must be feeling. Would her own mother worry and fret all night if *she* were missing?

14

LAYLA, *Saturday, April 13   9:45 p.m.*

"His iron claw made a circle of dead water round him,
from which they fled like affrighted fishes."
—from *Peter Pan*

The spinning hubcaps of Donovan's truck sparkled with raindrops.

"So, why you always gotta be the last one out?" Donovan said as he roared out of the parking lot.

Layla barely had time to buckle her seat belt. Her head bumped back into the padded headrest as the SUV swung into the street.

Layla exploded into tears.

"Dang, girl. What's up with you? Why you cryin'?"

"My mother is stupid, and my friend Diamond is missing," Layla choked out, gulping down a sob. She chose to leave her issues with *him* out of it.

"Diamond? The fine one?"

"Yeah." She paused. "Is that how you see her?"

"I'm not blind." He stopped at a red light, and Layla tried to pull herself together. Donovan nudged her with his shoulder. "Well, you can't fix stupid, and I'm sure Diamond will show up."

"You're no help," Layla muttered.

"Okay, okay. Calm down. Explain what you mean by *missing*," Donovan said.

Layla took a deep breath. "Diamond dipped out on the performance tonight. She said she had a chance to be in a movie, so she left with some dude she didn't even know."

"Huh. She came across to me as somebody with some sense."

"I just wanted to talk to her," Layla said, still sniffing.

"Who? Diamond?"

"No. My mother. She blew me off. She's got a *date*."

"Get back, Moms. Momma's gonna kick it tonight."

Layla glared at him. "I hate when she goes out. And she always picks some total lowlife."

"I guess even mothers have needs."

"She's got a husband."

"Who is locked up."

"But just for two more years!"

"You living in dreamland, girl. Your mom won't want your daddy when he gets out." He turned the windshield wipers up to a faster speed. They swished back and forth almost frenetically.

Layla sighed. "Maybe not. But it's *possible* they could work things out."

"Seems like your mother's got a thing for losers."

"Look, I can talk about my mother, but you can't."

Donovan held up one hand in apology. "My bad."

"Sometimes she brings her dates home," Layla admitted. "I hate that even more. Plus, we never talk anymore, me and my mom."

"You got me. You wanna talk to me?"

"You're sweet to offer, Donny. But this is complicated."

"Try me. I'm complicated too!"

Layla laughed, then studied him for a moment. "You won't like some of it," she warned.

"I promise I'll be cool."

"Promise?"

"Didn't I just say that? Now, go on, spit it out." Donovan was starting to sound annoyed, so Layla hurried to tell him what was on her mind.

"Well, okay, so I was a little shaky about going onstage because Diamond wasn't there," she began. "She's, like, my rock. She makes me feel like I can do anything just because she says so. And she's, like, seriously missing. Nobody has heard from her for hours."

"Yeah, and?"

"*And* I'm standing in the wings, trying to visualize my dance, and you come backstage and start yelling at me!"

"Don't make *me* the bad guy!"

Layla turned away from him. "I knew I couldn't talk to you about this."

"I'm cool. I'm cool. Go on."

She waited a moment, then said, "I needed you on my side tonight. Not hassling me. You've got me, body and soul, and you don't need to growl at me like I'm your dog on a leash."

"Okay. Okay. I guess I went a little overboard. But you looked so *good* in that costume, and I didn't want to share that with an auditorium full of people."

"I looked good?"

"Good enough to lick the plate."

"Then why did you say I was getting fat?"

"Can't you take a joke?"

"It wasn't funny to *me*. I think I messed up my dance because I was worried about you."

"You messed up?"

"Didn't you see me wipe out?"

"I went outside after your teacher chased me away. All those dances look the same to me anyway. Girls jumpin' all over the stage. I had to get some air."

"You're kidding, right? You missed my *dance?*" Layla asked incredulously.

"Turns out I didn't miss much, to hear you tell it."

"I thought you came to see me perform—to support me."

"I did. But by the time I got back to my seat, you were just leaving the stage. People were clapping, so I figured you did fine. You always do."

"So not one person I care about saw me dance." Layla slumped back into the seat.

"Get over yourself. I told you—I sat through most of that boring stuff for you. Anyway, wasn't that you in the back row in the second half of the show?"

"Yeah, probably."

"So cheer up. I did my part. You owe me."

"Owe you? What?"

"You know."

"Not tonight, Donny. I gotta get home."

"Why? Your mom is out. We've got all night."

"Don't you have to get to work?"

"I'll call in sick."

"I'm wiped, Donny. I just want to get some sleep."

"I thought you loved me."

"You know I love you."

"Soooooo . . ."

"Donny, don't be like this."

"I saw you checkin' out Justin backstage."

"Huh? What are you talkin' about?"

"You savin' it for him?"

"What? You trippin'! Justin means nothing to me. Why you always gotta go there?"

"I'm just sayin' . . ."

"Take me home, Donny. Please. Don't make me prove anything tonight. I need to be alone to think and rest. Please."

He stopped at another red light, reached over, and grabbed her left arm. Hard. His fingernails clawed into her skin.

Layla cried out. "You're hurting me," she whispered.

"Love hurts," he said sharply. He released her arm when the light changed. But his face was stone.

"I want to go home," she pleaded, rubbing her arm.

"Okay, you win," he said finally. "But remember, you owe me."

15

JUSTIN, *Saturday, April 13   10 p.m.*

". . . he had dreams and they were more painful than the dreams of other boys."
—from *Peter Pan*

"You hungry, Jus?" Justin's dad asked, peeking into his son's room. "You've been moping around since you got home."

"I had a sandwich earlier. I just feel kinda maxed out."

"You did great tonight—I got some good stuff to edit down for these college applications."

"Thanks, Dad." Justin picked at the blue plaid comforter he'd had on his bed since he was about six.

"Something bothering you?" His dad came in and sank into Justin's desk chair.

"It's just that—well, I was really missing Mom tonight," Justin admitted. "I remember telling her dudes don't get bouquets of roses . . ."

". . . and she'd bring them every time anyway!" his dad finished with a small laugh. "She really got into your performances."

"And the practices. And the costumes. And the pictures. I think she had that camera surgically implanted in her hand!" Justin smiled, remembering.

"She's at your shows in spirit," his dad reminded him.

"Now you sound like those old ladies at church," Justin groaned. "I feel her spirit, but I'd rather have her here." He played with his braids. "*And* her flowers!"

"Me too, Justin. Me too."

The silence between them was accentuated by the relentless rain outside. It was still so hard to talk about her, especially to his dad. It was like if he talked to his father about his mom, he made his *dad* even sadder. It'd been an entire year since that damn phone call, a year since the police had told them there'd been an accident. A stormy night. A drunk driver. And his mom was gone. So completely not fair.

"Can I ask you something, Dad?" Justin asked after a few minutes.

"Sure."

"Girls are so complicated."

"That's the question? Sounds like you've got that one figured out already."

"Nah, I don't understand them at all."

"Can you give me a for-instance?"

"Well, one of the girls at the studio—you know Diamond, right?"

"Yes, the one with the pretty hair and smile. You've done duets with her a couple of times, haven't you?"

"Yeah, she's fine, but that's not why I mention her. She, like, ran away or got kidnapped or something."

His father sat up straight. "Oh my God! How did that happen?"

"We're not sure. You know how girls gather in groups and gossip. They were huddling all evening. I stay around the edges and try to keep up."

His father nodded. "I feel you there."

"But the bottom line is, Diamond didn't show up for the performance tonight. She sent her friend a text that said she was trying out for a part in some movie, and she went off with some strange guy. Nobody has heard anything from her since."

"Is this a girl you have feelings for, Justin?"

"No. I mean, I like her all right, but she's not special like that. I just don't get how girls can be so dumb."

"Ah. Let me go dig out my book called *Why Women Do Stuff*."

"You need to write it, Dad. Guys my age could use it."

"The whole thing would be two hundred blank pages, kiddo. The real answer is, nobody knows!"

"Yeah, like Layla . . ."

"Poor kid, she had a rough night," his father commented.

"You saw her mess up?"

"She covered it quickly—very professionally, I thought."

"She's such a good dancer, but she doesn't think so." Justin sat up and let his long legs hang over the edge of the bed.

"How do you know?" his dad asked.

"No matter what compliment somebody gives her, she always talks down about herself."

"Confidence problem?"

"It's more than that, Dad. She's, like, really, really beautiful, but I don't think she sees that when she looks in the mirror."

"What does she see?"

"Somebody overweight and not good enough."

"Not good enough for what?"

"For dancing. For being. I think she sees herself as ugly."

"And what do you see?" He straightened a pile of books on Justin's desk.

Justin paused and pulled a sheet of notebook paper from the top drawer of his bedside table. He read slowly, giving each word its due. "She is beauty. She is grace. She moves like fluttering leaves."

"Wow. A girl who brings out the poetry in you."

"She *is* poetry to me."

"So why don't you tell her?"

Justin let the paper drift to the floor. "I can't."

His dad raised his eyebrows. "Why not?"

"She's all hooked up with somebody else."

"So what?"

"It's complicated, Dad."

"There's a girl you care about and you won't even let her know?"

"You remember Donovan, the kid I used to hang out with in elementary school? We used to be best friends. Not that you could tell now," Justin added.

Mr. Braddock shifted in his chair. "Yeah, cute little fellow. Smart. Loved cars, if I remember. What happened to you two, by the way?"

"He's not so little anymore. He's into some shady stuff, and he's got, like, these chains around Layla. She looks at him like he's the last player on the planet."

"That may be, but I've never known you to back away from a challenge."

Justin sighed. "It's like he controls her, like she's his toy that he winds up, and she does what he wants. She deserves so much better than that."

His father gave him a sidelong glance. "How do you know she's not happy being his toy?"

"How can anybody feel good about being used like that?"

His dad nodded. "You've got a point there."

"That's another chapter in your book, I guess." Justin stood up and scratched his head. "But really, Dad. Why would she stay with a dude like him? What's up with that?"

"Well, I suppose she has to want more for her life; she has to want to escape from a guy like Donovan."

"So how do I make *that* happen, Dad?"

"Just be yourself. Reach out to her if you can. Read my book."

Justin laughed. "Yeah, maybe I can add a chapter to it one day."

"Follow your heart, Justin. She'll figure out how much you care."

Justin began pacing around the bedroom. "Yeah, right. Easy for you to say."

"I've been around the block a couple of times."

"It's weird. Me and Donny used to be friends. But now he treats me like the enemy."

"My army buddies used to say, 'All's fair in love and war.' You willing to fight for the young lady?"

"I hope it doesn't come to that. But I sure wish she knew how I felt."

"She'll never know unless you tell her," his dad said, picking Justin's poem up off the floor, holding it out.

"Yeah, I know, I know. I'll think about it," Justin said, taking the paper.

"Good. Now get some sleep. I hope it works out for you." His father closed the door quietly behind him.

Justin sat on the edge of his bed, trying to make sense of his jumbled thoughts. Finally he turned off his lamp and slid under the covers. But it took a long, long time for him to fall asleep.

16

LAYLA, *Saturday, April 13   11 p.m.*

"Tink was not all bad: or, rather, she was all bad just now,
but, on the other hand, sometimes she was all good."
—from *Peter Pan*

Layla showered slowly, letting the warm water massage
her sore arm. She could already tell that she'd have to
wear long sleeves tomorrow. She toweled off carefully,
put on her pajamas, and picked up her phone. Scrolling
through her list, she tapped Mercedes' picture. Seconds
later Mercedes picked up.

"What's up, girl? Any news?" Layla asked, stretching
out on her bed.

"Nothing. And it's driving me bananas. My dad said the police think Diamond might have run away," Mercedes told her.

"No way. No *way*. Diamond would never do that. Now if you hear of *me* running away from *my* crazy mother, you better check the homeless shelters and parks. I might be under a bench!"

Mercedes laughed, then asked, "Are you hanging with Donovan tonight?"

"No, I sent him home. Too much drama for one night."

"Yeah, that dude does seem to bring it with him."

"Aw, girl, you just never get to see his sweet side. When we're alone, he's like a cuddly puppy." Layla wouldn't let herself think about the marks on her arm.

"He seems more like a pit bull to me."

"See what I mean? You gotta see it from my point of view. Donny is there for me when nobody else is around. He makes my heart beat fast when I just *look* at him. Plus, his ride is so tight. He let me drive it the other night. Whoa, that engine's got power!" Layla wanted her friend to understand, but she found it hard to put it all into words.

Mercedes wasn't getting it. "I think he loves that car more than you. You could do better. You know that, don't you?"

Layla fluffed her pillows behind her head. "How can I do better when I already have the best?"

"Okay, he's gorgeous. I give you that, but he's always got that frown on his face, like he's angry, like he's ready to bite somebody."

"It's just an act." Layla paused and touched her arm. "Look, he could be with any girl in school, but he chose *me*! I'm pretty lucky."

"You've got it backward, Layla. He should feel lucky have *you*."

"Why?"

"Look. Steve tells me all the time how great it is to be with *me*." Mercedes said. "He tells me that all the time."

"Did Steve tattoo your name on his arm?"

"He didn't have to; I don't need all that to know he cares about me."

"Donny paid a lot of money for that tattoo. If I had some cash, I'd surprise him and have his name inked right over my heart. Maybe I can do that for his birthday," Layla mused.

Mercedes' sigh from her end of the phone was explosive. "Don't you dare! Miss Ginger would have a cow!"

"Well, maybe I'll get the tat where Miss Ginger can't see it!" Layla replied.

"What if he breaks up with you?"

"That's never gonna happen."

"Be for real. This is high school. Everybody breaks up."

"Not me and Donny. Not if I keep him happy."

"That's the dumbest thing I ever heard, Layla," Mercedes practically shouted.

"Aren't you scared of losing Steve? Don't you work hard to keep him?"

"Hah! Steve works hard to keep *me*!"

Layla shifted the phone to her other ear. "I'm just sayin' . . ." She could feel herself getting annoyed, and

Mercedes must have sensed it, because she changed the subject.

"Hey, I meant to tell you—congratulations on getting the part of Wendy in the show."

Layla grinned. "Thanks. I can hardly believe it! I was sure Miss Ginger would choose Diamond."

"I think Diamond was a little bummed," Mercedes confided.

"Hey, you think that had something to do with why she ran off to be in the real movie version of *Peter Pan*?" Layla asked. "'Cause I'd rather she had the lead if that had anything to do with it. I don't deserve such a big part."

Mercedes gave an exasperated sigh. "Layla! Quit dissin' yourself. You're a great dancer, and you'll rock that role." Then she added slyly, "Plus, you get lots of cool dances with Justin."

"So what? Justin is just a dude who can dance."

Mercedes sighed once more. "Layla, you know that Justin likes you, don't you?"

"Justin?" Layla sniffed. "He likes to dance with me."

"Watch how he looks at you sometime."

"Who cares? I've got Donny. I don't need to look at anyone else."

Mercedes was quiet for a moment. Then Layla heard her say in a rush, "Donny does quite a bit of looking around sometimes. You should know that, Layla."

"I'm not gonna even listen to this."

Mercedes continued anyway. "Hey, look, I don't want to get you upset, but Steve told me that sometimes he sees

Donovan out cruisin' in that 'Lade with Magnificent Jones."

"He's lying!" Layla said dismissively, but she felt her stomach lurch. *No way. No way. No way.*

Magnificent Significant Jones (why her mama named her that, Layla could only guess) was almost six feet tall and had hips and boobs that jutted out like the rock faces on a climbing wall. She seemed to invite exploration. She didn't actually walk—she oozed down the school halls. She was like one of those Sirens Layla had read about in her Greek mythology book. Guys just stopped and melted when she passed by. Even the male teachers paused and made excuses to get a drink from the water fountain when Magnificent strolled through the halls.

"Layla, Steve wouldn't lie. You know that song by Adele called 'Rumour Has It'?"

"Yeah." Layla shifted uncomfortably as the words from the song rang through her head. Defiantly, she told Mercedes, "Girl, Donny *loves* me." But even as she was saying this, she was remembering silently agonizing over the balled-up McDonald's napkins on the floor of Donny's car. Napkins smeared with purple lipstick. Layla wore pink lipstick. Always.

"Has he ever told you that?"

Layla paused, stung. He hadn't, actually—not yet. And she had to admit that it was really starting to bother her. But she wasn't about to share that bit of info with Mercedes. So she said, "Well, duh! He calls me every night and tells me he loves me before I go to sleep."

"Just keep your eyes open, girlfriend. You hear?"

"Yeah, whatever," Layla replied in a huff. She was in

no mood to talk or think about Donovan and Magnificent anymore. So it was her turn to change the subject. "Hey, Mercedes."

"Yeah?"

"What do you think Diamond is doing right now?"

"Wishing she was at home in her own bed."

17

DIAMOND, *Saturday, April 13   11 p.m.*

"Why are you crying?"

—from *Peter Pan*

The door opened slowly. All she could see in the shaft of yellow light was Thane's silhouette. He entered the room.

"Thane! Oh my gosh— Help me! Untie me! What's going on?"

"Are you done crying?"

"Please! *Please* call my mother. I want to go home!"

"That's not going to happen." He laughed—and Diamond felt the coldness of it through her bones.

She fought to keep her voice under control, to keep the panicked sobs down. "My clothes—please, can I have my clothes?" She fought against the restraints. "I don't understand! Why am I tied up?"

Thane walked around the bed, his eyes never leaving her. "You said you wanted to be in a movie, didn't you?"

"Yes, but, I thought—"

"You thought you were coming to a casting call. And you are. Oh yes, you are," Thane said.

"But—but what about Chloe and the other girls? I'm so confused. I need my clothes. Please, please untie me!" Her head pounded, and her brain felt so fuzzy. She couldn't think. Why was the room spinning?

Thane laughed again. "You still don't get it, do you? You wanted to be in a movie, and you're just in time for your audition."

Diamond tried to think straight. Nothing made sense. She felt drugged. "Wha? What? I—I don't understand."

Thane flicked on the lights, and Diamond twisted her head away from the sudden brightness.

"You will be *the star* tonight, my dear girl," Thane whispered. Then, in a louder voice, he called, "Lights. Camera. Action."

Diamond blinked her eyes open, straining to see in the harsh, glaring light. Two large movie cameras were positioned directly over the bed. *Oh, no! Oh, no!* Her heart thudding, she jerked and thrashed against the ropes once more.

"No!" she screamed. "Let me go! Please, please, let me go!"

Thane ignored her. "Jimmy. Mickey. Come on in."

Diamond gasped as two huge men entered the room. The first, heavily bearded, wore a crisp, white sleeveless T-shirt—a sharp contrast to the coarse black hair that covered his arms. His arms were broad and burly. The other man, who was extremely overweight, was clean shaven. He wore a flowered Hawaiian shirt and plaid shorts.

"Meet my cameramen," Thane said genially.

The two men grinned at Diamond and took their places at the cameras, one at the foot of the bed, and one on the side.

Diamond's mind went in a dozen directions—she struggled through the haze of her cloudy thoughts. Slowly, she began to put together the pieces of what was happening. Oh, no. Oh, no. Oh, no.

Thane removed his pale yellow silk shirt and folded it carefully, then set it on the chair.

Diamond's eyes grew wide with horror. "Oh, no. Please, no. Please don't. You can't do this. I'm only fifteen," she begged softly. "Please."

"I can. And I will. Now relax and shut up—I'm very good at this."

He nodded to the two men. A red light blinked on the front of each camera.

Stunned into silence, Diamond finally understood the horrible enormity of her situation.

18

MERCEDES, *Sunday, April 14   11 a.m.*

"I don't see how it can have a happy ending."

—from *Peter Pan*

Mercedes sat in the seventh row of the congregational church, next to her mother. They always sat in row seven. Even though there were no names engraved on the back, Mercedes had noticed that church folk tended to take ownership of certain seats. Her mom had claimed the aisle seat on the seventh row many years ago. Visitors who made the mistake of sitting there before her mom arrived were glared at until they scooted over. Mrs. Ford would then offer her gloved hand and a broad smile in welcome.

Who still wears gloves to church? Mercedes thought. Then she just laughed the thought away because her mom dressed straight out of *Essence* magazine—perfectly coordinated and stylishly chic. Today she was decked out all in blue: a deep blue two-piece suit with a skirt that hit her legs exactly three inches below the knee—she never wore slacks to church—navy blue patent leather pumps with sensible two-inch heels, and the latest Coach purse. She always wore a hat—a big hat. For this particular Sunday morning, she'd chosen one with an elaborate blue brim and a bright pink feather. Mrs. Ford was *the* fashion statement of Sunday service.

Mercedes purposely wore slacks and sneakers. She'd tried to wear jeans a couple of times, but her mom had acted like she was about to die of a heart attack or maybe embarrassment. Either way, Mercedes had rolled her eyes, but changed her clothes.

The service was quiet. Peaceful hymns, controlled prayers, and a sensible sermon. But Mercedes wanted to, needed to, scream. She could have really used a good, old-fashioned holy-roller church today. She yearned for a hundred-voice choir dressed in red robes to holler and sing, an amped-up organ to blast the beat with the singers, booming drums to pound, and a preacher who shouted and sweated and prayed for Diamond to come home.

Instead Mercedes sat next to her impeccably poised mother while another polite hymn was sung in perfect harmony. She'd grown up in this church, and in spite of her rebellion against what she told her mother was "mind-boggling boredom," she knew how to find that quiet place within herself. She'd never let her mother know, of course, but she had found how to let herself be carried by the serene melodies to a place where she could do her own praying. She didn't think of God as some bearded guy in the sky. God was like a person she felt like she could talk to.

So, rather than let her head explode in frustration, she bowed her head and sought that place. *Lord, please forgive me for letting Diamond get kidnapped. Friends are supposed to protect friends from bad guys, right? I hope this isn't out of line, but where were You? How come You let this happen? I'm not blaming You, but couldn't You have whipped up an earthquake or something—just enough to make her think that maybe getting into that car was a really bad idea?*

She needs Your help, Lord. Can You whisper to her that we're all looking for her, that we all care about her? Can You give her some kind of heavenly hug that lets her know she's not alone and that there's hope? There is hope for her, right? I know You've been getting lots of prayers about Diamond lately. I guess folks clog Your in-box all the time with stupid prayers for dumb stuff. But this is real and serious. Please let Diamond come home safe. Please?

Mercedes' mother nudged her. "Wake up."

"I'm not asleep," Mercedes whispered.

The congregation rose for the final hymn and prayer. Well-dressed, hat-wearing women like her mother and casually dressed ladies in flip-flops. Fidgety, probably

100

hungry, children. Men looking dapper in white shirts and dark suits and red striped ties, as well as men in golf shirts and khakis. Teenagers in shorts and T-shirts. Old ladies with walkers. Young married couples with squirming babies.

Her father, who was the newly appointed youth pastor, stepped up to the pulpit and took the mike from the lead pastor, who handed it to him with a nod. "I'd like to make a special request this morning," Mr. Ford explained. "Please join hands." Everyone looked around in confusion. This was not part of Sunday service.

He waited until hands linked. "As we leave this place of worship," he began, "let us all be thankful for the gifts of God. And let us also be mindful of a gaping hole in our midst. All of you, I'm sure, have heard about the disappearance of a young woman from our community. Let us bow our heads and pray for her now, and I ask that you continue to pray for her from your homes." He took a deep breath. "Dear Lord, we ask that You keep Diamond Landers in Your arms of protection and bring her home quickly and safely to her family. Amen."

Mercedes looked up in surprise as the whole church erupted with a loud and hearty "Amen." *Maybe this prayer stuff is gonna work.*

19

DIAMOND, *Sunday, April 14   10 a.m.*

"Hook wounded me. I can neither fly nor swim."
—from *Peter Pan*

Pain, searing pain, woke Diamond up the next morning. She was covered by a thin sheet that only came up to her waist. She felt like she would vomit. Still tied to the bed, but by only one arm this time, she groaned as she pulled the sheet the rest of the way up to hide her nakedness. Every muscle ached, bringing back the horrible details of the night before. She couldn't stop crying. She wanted her mother, her father, her sister, the warmth and safety of home. It hurt. It hurt so much.

And she felt so ashamed.

And furious! Thane, that evil, lying monster, was holding her prisoner. She was—oh God! He'd *kidnapped* her! She had no idea where she was or how to get away. And it was her own stupid fault. Stupid stupid stupid fault. She thrashed and screamed and clawed at the rope, but it did not budge—the knot would not give. She lay there finally, quiet, trembling, overwhelmed with terror, trying to keep her mind from imagining what he would do next.

The door opened suddenly, and Thane entered carrying a tray. He smiled broadly. "Good morning, my princess! I brought you breakfast." He carefully closed and locked the door behind him.

Diamond pulled her knees to her chest, pain surging through her. "Will you let me go now? I won't tell anyone, I swear. Please just let me go," she pleaded, covering her face with her free arm.

"Oh, I wouldn't hear of it, my dear. You are a star! Your movie debut was amazing!"

Diamond thought she was going to gag. "Please, please let me go home. I'll never tell. Never!"

Instead of answering her, Thane walked over to the bed and untied her arm. Diamond flinched as he began to gently rub where the ropes had gouged angry red marks into her wrist. "Go on and take a shower; the bathroom is right over there. You'll feel a lot better. I've got fresh clothes laid out for you, and then you can eat."

Diamond was too scared not to do what he asked. She let him help her sit up, let him carefully wrap the sheet around her, then walked with him to the small bathroom. Each step sent pain flashing through her abdomen. Her mind was racing—should she try to fight him now that her hands were free? Make a run for it? To where—the locked door? He'd catch her, and what then? What if he got mad? What if he tried to kill her?

She couldn't risk it—not yet—she had no chance right now. Despondent, she let herself be led into the bathroom. Thane turned on the shower, then closed the door and left her alone. Diamond looked around wildly, but the bathroom, of course, had no window. There was no lock on the door either. Who didn't have a lock on a bathroom door? Heart sinking, she stood in the shower for what seemed like an hour, trying in vain to wash the stench of last night's nightmare from her body.

When the water turned cold, she toweled off, but she still felt filthy. Wincing, she put on the clothes Thane had left for her—underwear, jeans, and T-shirt that, weirdly, fit perfectly, and peeked into the bedroom. He was gone.

She stepped back into the room, noticing that he had changed the sheets and fluffed the pillows. A breakfast of a banana, orange juice in a Styrofoam cup, and a Krispy Kreme doughnut sat on a tray decorated with one red rose lying on a napkin. Diamond stared at the rose, then flung it away against the far wall. What a pig! What a . . . Wait! Utensils! Maybe there was a fork—she could use a fork as a weapon! She pulled aside the napkin. There were no utensils.

Diamond tried the door. Locked. She pounded on it, kicked it with all her might, beat it until her hands were sore. She screamed, "Let me out of here! You can't do this! Let me go! Please! I want to go home!"

But all was silent.

Exhausted, she sat down and paid close attention to where she was. The room was small, the walls steeply slanted. It made her feel a little dizzy to look at them. A converted attic, she figured. The only window, a small octagon, was tucked at least twenty feet above her head, in the triangle where the two walls met. A chance to escape? Probably not. How would she ever get up there? Thin light, made gray by the rainy weather, filtered through it.

She paced the room, checking for anything she could use to help her. She tried to remove a picture from the wall, but found it was nailed there. There were no lamps. No decorations. No television. There was nothing she could use as a weapon. Not one thing. She put her ear to the door, but she all she could hear was thick silence. It was as if she were in a tomb.

The cameras had been removed, she noticed, but the massive, heavy-duty tripods stood poised and ready, permanently attached to the floor. She could not budge either one. The dresser drawers were nailed shut. The single chair was bolted to the floor. She swung open the closet door. It was empty.

The deeply angled walls felt as if they were closing in on her. She spun around, beating on the walls, screaming up at the distant window. She screamed and yelled and begged until her throat was raw and raspy.

Finally, bleakly, she sipped a bit of the orange juice.

She figured she needed to keep herself strong if she ever had any chance of escape.

She sat on the chair, curling her knees up to her chin. There was no way she going to sit on that bed. The only sound Diamond could hear was the rain and wind against the tiny window.

As she picked at the striped upholstery of the chair, she couldn't stop thinking of her parents. Her sister. Were they looking for her? Did they think she'd run away? They'd come looking for her, right? With a pang, she realized no one had any inkling of where to start a search. Like a bubble, Diamond had simply vanished.

She started to cry, softly, emptily, dreading the coming night.

20

MERCEDES, *Sunday, April 14   3 p.m.*

"She is an abandoned little creature."
—from *Peter Pan*

Sunday dinner at Mercedes' house was supertraditional. "I think I have the only mother in the universe who still cooks Sunday dinner," she'd once told Diamond. "Fried chicken. Mashed potatoes. Green beans. Chocolate cake. On real plates—not paper ones."

"You can get the same thing at KFC," Diamond had replied, licking the icing off a thick slice of cake that Mercedes had brought for lunch. "But not like this. Yum. Your mom rocks!"

"My mom has issues," Mercedes had responded, laughing.

"Don't they all?"

"She keeps the spices in alphabetical order. Canned goods are stacked by size of can, then by ingredients. Don't even ask about the bathroom!"

Diamond had laughed. "I've seen your bathroom. Red towels on the left. Blue washcloths on the right. Does she count sheets of toilet paper?"

"Probably! Me and my dad just go with the flow."

"I wonder if it's hereditary," Diamond had said pensively.

"I guess a little OCD comes in handy when you're trying to keep a busy house in order. But when I get my own place, I'm gonna keep everything in the middle of the floor and just dig for stuff when I need it!"

"That's gonna drive your mom crazy," Diamond had said, laughing again.

"I know. I love it!"

Mercedes smiled as she finished up the dishes with her mother, thinking about the last time Diamond came over.

"What do you think about the candlelight vigil the school has planned?" her mom asked. "It's a little soon, don't you think?"

Mercedes frowned. "I don't know. I guess people feel like they gotta do *something*," she replied. "I mean, there's not much else we can actually *do*. I just feel like I'm gonna throw up, you know?" She slammed a stack of spoons noisily into the drawer.

Her mother dried her hands quickly and pulled

Mercedes toward her. "They will find her, baby girl. They just have to."

Mercedes melted into her mom's damp, soap-smelling arms. "Will you and Daddy come to the vigil?"

"Absolutely."

"Thanks, Mom," Mercedes said softly. After a moment she pulled away and said, "I think I'll run over to Diamond's house for a minute."

"You don't want to get in the way, honey."

"I won't, but maybe there's something I can do to help."

"Well, I made an extra cake to bring over tomorrow, but why don't you take it now? Give me a minute to frost it," her mother said. "And I get it—wanting to do something. I don't know what else to do but pray and cook."

Mercedes ended up loading her car with a large box that held the cake, plus a full meal in a half dozen little plastic containers, which her mother kept, of course, neatly stacked, sized, and color coded. And she realized that those little containers were order. Somewhere, there was order. She started the car feeling more hopeful than she had all day.

But when she got to Diamond's house, she was stunned by all the activity. Three police cars were parked in the driveway. Several police officers huddled on the front lawn.

A television news van with a huge satellite extending from the top of it was positioned two doors down.

Yellow crime-scene tape encircled the yard. *Why the drama tape?* Mercedes thought. *It's not like a crime happened here*. Maybe it was just to keep the crowd away—a good-size group of people, maybe neighbors, maybe just nosy folks who'd heard the story on the news, hovered just outside the tape. Many had their cameras and cell phones out.

What do they think they'll get a picture of? Mercedes thought, getting angry. *Diamond's cat? Her front door?*

More police patrolled the taped area, warning onlookers to keep back.

She opened her door, then hesitated, not sure what to do or say. Grabbing the box of food items, she slammed her car door and then stomped up to the first police officer she saw. She didn't wait for him to try to keep her out.

"My name is Mercedes Ford. I am Diamond's best friend. I am delivering this box for my mother, and I need to get into that house right now."

The officer was unimpressed. "Driver's license, ma'am."

Mercedes wasn't sure whether to be thrilled or annoyed to be called ma'am, but she set the box down, pulled her wallet from her purse, and handed over her license.

He examined it as if she might have been a criminal on the loose. Even though it was broad daylight, he took out his flashlight and peered at the license more closely.

Just as she was about to lose her patience, Mercedes heard a small voice yell out her name. "Mercedes! Mama says come in! Hurry!"

The officer turned to see Shasta peeking out the front door. Cameras clicked at the movement and sound. Shasta disappeared in a hurry.

The policeman returned Mercedes' license and lifted the yellow tape so that she could enter the yard. She was aware of being filmed and photographed as she made a quick dash to the house. Instead of entering through the front door, she went in the side entrance, the kitchen door she always used when she visited.

Once inside, she breathed a sigh of relief. She went to place the food on the counter, but found there was barely enough room for her box. Dozens of store-bought cakes and pies, casserole dishes, soda bottles, and boxes of KFC chicken were already piled high, so she set her box on the kitchen table.

Mrs. Landers, her hair uncombed, her face blotchy, her eyes red, grabbed Mercedes and hugged her close. She began to weep. Mercedes found herself crying as well.

"Thank you for coming," Mrs. Landers said, grabbing a paper towel and wiping her eyes. "It's so good to see you. You give me hope."

"I'm so sorry, Mrs. L." Mercedes' voice wavered. "I . . . I feel like I'm to blame here. We shoulda stayed together."

"Oh, Mercedes. Please don't give yourself that burden." Diamond's mom hugged her even tighter. "A horrible, horrible person did this. Not you."

"Yeah, but I don't know how else to feel."

Mrs. Landers stepped back and took Mercedes' hands in hers. "We need your strength—maybe your brainpower."

"Huh?"

"You're a teenager. You and Diamond think a lot alike. Where would you go? What would you do if you were caught in something . . . terrible? We've got profilers here who might like to talk to you."

"I'll do anything! Just tell me . . ." She paused and pointed to the box. "My mom, uh, sent food."

Mrs. Landers' shoulders sank. "Please thank her. I appreciate all of this, I really do, but this stuff is what you send for a funeral! And she's not dead! My Diamond is not dead!" She leaned against a counter and started sobbing anew.

Shasta ran into the room, plucked a Kleenex from the box, and handed it to her mom. "Daddy needs you upstairs in Diamond's room," she told her. "The police want to check Diamond's computer."

Mrs. Landers mumbled something incoherent and hurried out of the room.

Mercedes turned to Shasta, who was looking at her with big, hopeful eyes. "So, how you holdin' up, Miss Shasta?" Mercedes asked.

"Not so good," the little girl admitted.

"Can we go hide in your room?" Mercedes asked.

"Okay. I think that's the only place in the house the police haven't turned upside down—yet."

As they headed for the stairs, Mercedes counted three policemen in the living room and two more in the den. Phones rang. Strange wires had been stretched across the floor. A bulky piece of electronic equipment sat on the dining room table next to a set of telephones.

"That stuff is for in case the kidnappers call for ransom—so they can trace the call," Shasta whispered.

"How do you know all this?"

"I listen at the top of the stairs."

When they reached Shasta's room, Shasta closed the door and locked it. Mercedes looked around. She'd never actually been in it—she'd only ever given it a quick glance on her way to Diamond's room. It was done in little-girl pink, with ponies and Barbie dolls and sparkly decorations on the walls. All the walls except for one. Black crayon and marker had been scribbled all over that one, at least the bottom four and a half feet of it that Shasta had been able to reach. Deep black streaks of black Magic Marker. Jagged circles and swirls. Thick, angry lines of black crayon.

Shasta plopped down on a pale pink beanbag chair. Her bed was unmade, the sheets in a pile on the floor.

Mercedes sat in the desk chair. "Interesting decorating style," she said, nodding toward the wall.

"I got mad."

"I see. Did it help?"

"Not really."

"Did your mom see this yet?"

"She wouldn't notice. Mama's living in crazy land. Daddy too."

"It's pretty bad, huh?"

"Mama keeps throwing up. And crying. Daddy breaks things."

"That must be a little frightening," Mercedes ventured.

Shasta shook her head. "You know what's a really scary thing to see?"

"What?"

"My daddy crying."

Mercedes reached over and gently touched Shasta's cheek. "What about you?"

Shasta started to cry. "I did something bad." She hiccupped.

Mercedes moved over and squatted beside her, alarmed. "What did you do, Shasta?"

"Mama and Daddy are gonna be so mad." She cried harder.

"What? You can tell me," Mercedes said gently.

Shasta looked through teary eyes at her, then over at the pile of sheets on the floor.

"I wet the bed last night."

Mercedes felt relief surge through her. "Oh, sweetie-girl, that's okay. Really."

"I haven't done that since I was, like, two years old!" Shasta admitted, covering her face with her fingers.

"Shhh. Shhh. Shhh. We'll just put some clean sheets on your bed. No big deal."

"What if I mess up again tonight?"

"Then I'll come over and help you again tomorrow."

Shasta stopped crying and gave her a baleful look. "You won't tell my mama?"

"Pinky promise. Plus, she's got enough on her mind."

Mercedes found some bright yellow sheets in a hall closet and swiftly changed Shasta's bed. She smoothed the blankets and patted the pillows, then motioned Shasta to climb up.

"Smells good," Shasta said.

"Yeah, I like clean sheets. Maybe they'll help you sleep better tonight."

"Probably not, if Diamond isn't home yet."

"She'll come home soon."

"How do you know?"

"Because she loves you, and she knows you're worried about her."

"Remember when I asked if I could come to the mall with you and Diamond?"

"Yeah."

"If I had been there, Diamond wouldn't be missing." Shasta started wailing. "She wouldn't have left me alone in the food court."

"She never would have—you're right. But you can't beat yourself up over what happened. That's what everybody keeps telling me."

"Nobody thinks a food court in a mall is dangerous," Shasta said. "Except sometimes the food is nasty."

"True that."

They sat in silence for a few minutes, then Shasta said, "Mama said I can't go to dance class. She won't even let me go to school tomorrow."

"She's just being careful. Are you all coming to the candlelight vigil tonight?" Mercedes asked.

"Yeah. We'll be there." Shasta paused. "Uh, Mercedes, can I ask you something?"

"Sure."

"What's a vigil? Everybody keeps talking about it, but . . . I was afraid to ask. It sounds kinda scary."

Mercedes pulled Shasta close. "It's where all of Diamond's friends will gather tonight to pray for her safe return. It should be nice."

"Okay. Thanks. All I knew was that it was outside, in the dark."

Mercedes gave her a hug. "Hey, you want something to eat? There's good food downstairs."

Shasta shook her head. "I'm not hungry."

"Not even for my mom's chocolate cake?"

Shasta gave a little giggle. "Well, maybe a little."

Mercedes left Shasta scribbling in a notebook rather than on the walls. At the bottom of the steps, she ran into Mrs. Landers.

"Mercedes, one of the officers wants to speak with you—he's a computer expert and profiler."

"Sure, anything to help."

Diamond's mother led her toward a youngish-looking man with sandy brown hair. He offered his hand to Mercedes. "Thanks for speaking to me. I'm Officer Rockside, and I'd like to ask you a few questions."

He motioned for her to sit at a chair in the dining room, where Diamond's Dell laptop with the custom-made rose-covered cover lay on the table, cords running to and from it. It was attached to a larger computer, which the police must have set up.

Diamond would sizzle if she knew someone was going through her personal stuff—her e-mails, her Facebook postings, her online history—was Mercedes' first thought.

"What are you looking for on Diamond's computer?" she asked.

"Any kind of clue that might help us find her. You and Diamond are pretty close friends, right?"

"Yeah, we've been tight since grade school."

"Would you know if she'd been talking to someone online, someone not in your usual circle of friends?"

"Yes, I would, and she wasn't!"

"How can you be sure?"

"We tell each other everything."

"Everything?"

"Yeah, pretty much."

"Are you aware she'd been talking on Facebook to someone named Justin Braddock?"

Mercedes had to stifle a smirk. "He's a guy in our dance class. He goes to our school; he's our friend."

The officer didn't respond, but jotted a few lines in his notebook. "So you know him?"

"I just told you. He's in our class at Crystal Pointe Dance Academy. If she's texted or e-mailed him, it was dance-related. There's nothing going on there. Besides, he likes another girl at the studio."

"Her name, please?" His pencil was poised.

"Layla Ridgewood."

He looked up then and asked, "Do you and Diamond text each other much?"

"All the time. Practically twenty-four-seven."

"May I have permission to look at your cell phone and check your past text messages?"

"If it will help find Diamond, you can download every stupid message I've ever sent or received in my whole life. But you won't find anything. We're just high school kids keepin' up with each other. We don't talk to weirdos."

Again, he wrote more notes. "Do you spend much time online?"

"Me? Yeah, I guess."

"What kind of sites do you visit?"

"Music sites. Games. Movie stars and singers. Looking up stuff for school. The usual." Even though she'd never done anything out of the ordinary on her computer, Mercedes suddenly felt uncomfortable with the policeman's questions. What if she had clicked on something wrong by accident?

"Do you have a Facebook page?"

"Yes."

"Do you post regularly?"

"Yeah, pretty much every day. It's kinda how we keep in touch with our friends. Texting and Facebook."

"Do you tweet? Or follow the tweets of people other than your friends at school?"

"A little. Sometimes I actually talk to real people!"

Officer Rockside laughed at that. "Me too." Then he asked Mercedes abruptly, "Do you have a boyfriend?"

Mercedes frowned impatiently. "Yes, but what does that have to do with anything?"

"His name, please?"

"Steve. Steve Wilkins. He's a senior at our school. Why are you asking me all this? They asked me all this stuff yesterday."

"Bear with me, please. I'm trying to get a feel for Diamond's life. If we understand you, her best friend, it will help us to understand Diamond, and maybe that information will assist us in finding her."

Mercedes couldn't contain herself. "Maybe if you'd actually *look* for her, you'd have a better chance of finding her than sitting here asking me questions!" she cried.

Officer Rockside ignored her outburst and calmly went on to the next question. "Does Diamond have a boyfriend?"

"Not right now. She broke up with a guy when school started last fall, and she hasn't really settled on anyone since. She doesn't date a lot, but she's been to parties and danced with a couple of dudes."

"I'll need their names, if you don't mind."

Mercedes sighed and shifted in her seat. "The guy she broke up with was Pierre Dennis. Turned out Pierre was going out with three other girls while he was supposed to be exclusive with Diamond. The girls met at a party one night, and all four of them dumped him the next day. It was kinda funny."

"So she wouldn't be charmed by this Pierre fellow if he'd contacted her online or by text?"

"Not a chance."

"And the others?"

"Nobody special, really. She stays busy with her dancing and her schoolwork. We dance four or five nights a week. When we get home from dance, we do our homework and collapse. We don't have time to look for dudes online!"

The officer scribbled something, then continued. "We've read the text she sent you. Is Diamond a big fan of California Clover and Diva Dawson?"

"Not any more than anybody else. They're our age, and they've made it big, so we admire them, but it's not like we're fan stalkers or anything."

"So you don't think Diamond would run away to be in a movie with either of those movie stars?"

"Look, Diamond did *not* run away," Mercedes insisted, her voice rising. "She was *not* lured away by some pedophile online. Somehow, somebody convinced her she could be in a movie, and she's with that person now. Look, I don't mean to be rude, but why don't you quit asking me dumb questions and go out there and find her?"

Officer Rockside's eyes grew kind. "Miss Ford, I understand your frustration. I can assure you that we have a team scouring the mall and that parking lot. We have a team checking video surveillance tapes in the area. We have officers looking for anyone who has recently rented movie equipment. We are using every means at our disposal to find your friend, and the answers to your questions can actually help us."

Mercedes took this all in, willing herself to calm down. "Did you find out if a studio is filming a movie in the area? Wouldn't it be on the news if Diva Dawson and California Clover were in town?" she asked.

A shadow crossed Officer Rockside's face. "I probably shouldn't tell you this, but California Clover is in London, and we've tracked Diva Dawson to Brazil. Both are on location and have been for several weeks." He paused, then added, "Neither of them has anything scheduled for this area."

Mercedes felt her heart grow icy, and let out a groan. "Uh, well, thanks for letting me know," she finally said.

The policeman rose and closed his notebook. "I

appreciate your candor. I hope your friend is found soon. We're doing our best. Trust me."

Mercedes stood up, feeling shaky, and found her way to the kitchen to make a sandwich for Shasta. She added a piece of her mom's cake to the plate, then poured a glass of milk.

As she trudged back up the stairs, she wondered how the heck she'd manage to keep cheerful and upbeat in front of Diamond's little sister.

"Hey, I cut you a slice with the thickest frosting," she told Shasta as she entered the room. "And I made you a sandwich—your mom needs you to be strong and healthy. You don't want her to worry about you being sick on top of everything else, do you?"

Shasta took a bite, then set the sandwich down. "I heard you downstairs."

"What?"

"Talking to the cop."

Mercedes' mind churned as Shasta reminded her that she hid at the top of the stairs to get info. How much of that conversation would a nine-year-old have understood? she wondered.

"You probably shouldn't have done that," was all Mercedes could manage to say.

"That's the only way I find out anything around here!" Shasta shoved the plate away, hitting it into the milk and spilling it. "Diamond's never coming home, is she?" she asked, her voice fierce.

Mercedes didn't know what to say. She was worried about exactly the same thing.

21

LAYLA, *Sunday, April 14   6 p.m.*

"It's all a bit tragic, really, isn't it?"
—from *Peter Pan*

Layla whipped off a text to Mercedes about the vigil, then flopped on the faded flowered sofa. She picked up the remote, but tossed it aside—she didn't think she could handle the noise of the overly cheerful television commercials that encouraged everyone to buy this tooth-paste or that pasta or that sleek new car.

Layla and her mom had moved to their small apart-ment shortly after her father had been sent to prison.

Those four rooms had seen many occupants. The floors and woodwork were scuffed, the walls needed a coat of paint, and the faucet in the kitchen dripped all night. But they kept everything dusted and the furniture polished, and Layla made sure the yellow curtains in the kitchen window stayed clean and fresh. She wasn't much of a housekeeper in her own bedroom, but she kept the kitchen spotless.

One of the best conversations she remembered having with her dad was in the kitchen of their old house. It had been a big, rambling house, also old, but not sad and ragged like their apartment. The house had what her father had called "character," with a porch that wrapped around the whole building. She'd played on that porch every day in the summer. It had been a puppet show backdrop, a racetrack, and a modeling runway. And, of course, a practice stage for her dancing.

"They don't build houses like this anymore," her dad had told her. He'd been sipping a tall lemonade from an icy glass while glancing at the newspaper at the kitchen table. "This house was built to be a home, a place where a family can always feel safe. "

"I always feel safe with you around, Daddy," Layla had said to him, climbing onto his lap. He had smelled yummy— he had worn a leathery lemon-tinged cologne. Now, whenever she sipped lemonade, she thought of her dad.

"See those curtains?" he'd said, nodding toward the ones in the kitchen.

"Yeah."

"When I come home from work and see you dancing

like a pretty little bird on our big ol' porch, and I see those yellow curtains doin' their own dance in the breeze, I know I'm home with my girls and everything is fine, just fine."

When Layla and her mother were forced to leave the house with the wonderful porch because they simply could no longer afford it, they had to leave much of their furniture and many of their belongings behind. Who needs a lawnmower or a snow shovel when you're living in an apartment? But Layla, even though she had only been ten years old, carefully took down those kitchen curtains and swore to herself that when her father got home, those yellow curtains would be waiting for him.

Whether her *mom* would be waiting was another question. She knew her mother rarely made the five-hour drive to where her father was being held, and they hardly ever talked on the phone. Jail phone calls were crazy expensive for both parties.

Thinking about jail cells made Layla remember that Diamond was out there somewhere. Maybe being kept against her will. Maybe scared and alone. She wrapped her arms around her knees, hoping against hope that she wasn't.

When the phone rang, she jumped. The ringer sounded muffled, so she followed the noise until she found the phone—stuffed in the junk drawer in the kitchen.

"Hello?"

When she pulled the phone from the drawer, the

phone bill, the light bill, and a folded sheet of paper all came out with it, tumbling to the floor.

"Hey, Layla. Uh, this is Justin."

"Hi, Justin. What's up? Why you calling on the home phone?"

"Oh, my bad. I meant to call your cell."

Layla reached down to stick the bills and the letter back in the drawer. Her mom had one strange filing system, she thought.

"I just wanted to let you know I thought you did a great job at the showcase last night."

"You're kidding, right? Didn't you see me splat my fat butt all over the stage?"

"I think you handled it gracefully and professionally. It happens to all of us. You ever watch *Dancing with the Stars*? They wipe out all the time, and they're on national television!"

"Well, I'm glad there were no cameras last night!" Layla paused. The folded letter had fallen open. The heading read, in large black letters, BUREAU OF CORRECTIONS.

"You know, you look awesome every time you dance," Justin told her.

Layla picked the letter up distractedly, hardly noticing the nervousness in Justin's voice.

"Huh? Oh, thanks." Layla quickly scanned the letter.

"Are you there? Do we have a bad connection?" Justin asked. "My cell phone is funky, and sometimes I have trouble getting enough bars for a signal."

"What? No. I mean, I'm here. I got sidetracked—I just was reading a letter I found."

"A letter? Are you okay? You sound shaky."

"Yes, I am. I mean, no, I'm not. I don't know." Layla stuffed the letter back in the drawer, her hand trembling.

"What's wrong, Layla? Tell me."

Layla hedged. "Well, it's, like, uh . . . I guess everybody knows my father is in jail."

"Yeah, so?"

"I just found this letter in the kitchen drawer. It's from two weeks ago."

"What's it say?"

Layla shook her head in disbelief. "I can't believe my mother didn't tell me!"

"Tell you what?"

"My dad—he's coming home—this week! My daddy's coming home!"

"That's great news, Layla! You must be so psyched."

"Maybe my mom wanted to surprise me," she said, wondering why her mother hadn't told her yet— Why hadn't she?

"That would be so cool," Justin offered. His voice sounded cautious, as if he weren't sure exactly what to say.

"But . . . maybe she's ashamed of him. Maybe she won't want him in the house. She wouldn't do that, would she? Not let me see him? Maybe that's why she didn't tell me!"

"I don't know. All I know is I'd give anything to see my mom again. You're really lucky, Layla."

"Oh, Justin. I'm sorry. I forgot about your mother. Jeez—I've been feeling sorry for myself for the past six years because I didn't have my father with me, and for you, that pain is forever."

"Yeah, it kinda is," he replied, his voice getting husky. Then he asked, "Are you coming to the candlelight vigil for Diamond tonight?"

"Of course! Donny's picking me up in a few."

"Uh, yeah, right. I guess I'll see you there, then," Justin said.

"Hey, I gotta go, Justin. I've got to wash the kitchen curtains."

"Huh? Tonight?"

"It's a private thing between me and my dad. And I have to call Donny and tell him the good news! I'll see you tonight at the vigil. Bye!"

She hung up before Justin had finished saying good-bye.

22

JUSTIN, *Sunday, April 14   8 p.m.*

". . . the world was round, and so in time they must come back to their own window."
—from *Peter Pan*

In spite of the chilly drizzle, the crowd surrounding the flagpole at Broadway High grew from just a few students to a huge throng in a matter of minutes. Huddled five and six deep, whispering softly, many held umbrellas, so from a distance, the group looked like a multicolored cloud.

Justin carried no umbrella. He wore a thick black

hoodie, which he knew would be soaked by the end of the evening, but he didn't care.

The principal, Mrs. Gennari, in the brightest green raincoat he had ever seen, passed out candles and paper plates. Justin was glad to see that his father had come, and he noticed Layla's mom in the crowd as well. Mercedes' mom was helping pass out the candles, while her dad had gone to talk to the news crew that had materialized out of the darkness.

"Stay back and show some respect," Mr. Ford was saying. "This is a vigil, not a breaking news story. You understand?"

The reporter nodded, but moved to a prime position anyway.

"Punch a hole in center of the paper plate," Mrs. Gennari was explaining, "and push your candle through. That way you won't get burned by the melting wax. But please be careful with the flames. I can't deal with any more trauma this weekend."

Jillian glided over to Justin, her movements fluid even when she wasn't dancing. She handed him a red ribbon, pinned in the middle. "Wear it for Diamond," she told him.

"You made all these?" Justin asked in surprise, looking at the shoebox full of ribbons she held.

"I couldn't sleep," she said with a shrug. She moved to another group of students and gave each of them a ribbon as well.

There were lots of kids from the dance studio in the crowd, as well as Miss Ginger and nearly all Diamond's teachers from school.

Zizi was passing out flyers. Each one had Diamond's picture on it, and the words, HAVE YOU SEEN THIS GIRL? PLEASE CALL 800-555-3344 IF YOU HAVE ANY INFORMATION. More details, like police phone numbers and e-mail contact information, filled the bottom of the flyer.

When Diamond's parents, looking both drained and tense, arrived and joined the crowd, people reached out to touch them. To show their support, Justin guessed. Shasta, her eyes large and frightened, clung to her mother's hand.

Mercedes hurried over to them and led them to a few chairs that had been set up inside the circle, close to the flagpole. Mrs. Landers thanked her, looking grateful for a place to sit.

Justin heard Donovan's car before he saw it. The engine rumbled and the music blared—loud and disrespectful, Justin thought. A few minutes later he saw Layla and Donny join the crowd, holding hands.

Jillian hurried over to give them ribbons. Layla pinned hers to her jacket. Donny glanced at the slim red ribbon, then stuffed it into his pocket.

As one by one, everyone began to light their candles, the tiny sparks of light seemed to converge into a huge, glowing blossom of fire, a ring of incandescence in the darkness.

When it seemed that all the candles were lit and all those who were coming had assembled, Mrs. Gennari asked for their attention over her portable microphone. "We are here tonight to show our support to Diamond's family and to pray for her safe return. We want Diamond to know, wherever she is, that we love her and just want her to be back here with us. We'd like to ask Mr. Ford, who is the youth pastor of the Broadway Avenue Congregational Church, to say a few words."

Justin noticed a small smile on Mercedes' face as all eyes looked to her father.

"The Bible tells the story," the pastor began, "of a man who had a hundred sheep and lost one of them. He left the ninety-nine and went looking for that one lost sheep. And when he found it, he called his friends and neighbors and celebrated. That's what we're going to do when Diamond comes home."

"You throwin' the party?" someone asked from the crowd.

"I'd be glad to," Mr. Ford replied. "We'll have it at the church."

The voice from the crowd didn't reply. Justin figured that that wasn't the kind of party he'd been looking for.

"Let us pray," Pastor Ford continued. "Dear Lord, please be with Diamond tonight. Let her know we love her. Let her know we care. Please keep her safe from harm and bring her back safely so we can rejoice. Amen."

"Amen," many of the students murmured.

"Would anyone like to add something?" Mrs. Gennari asked. She held up the portable microphone.

Justin was surprised to see that Layla was the first to raise her hand. Mrs. Gennari nodded to her.

Layla began to speak, her voice shaky. Justin thought the flickering light from the candle made her face look almost angelic. "Diamond is my friend," she said, "and

I believe with all my being that she is coming home. I gotta believe that. I gotta believe that." She started to cry and, leaning into Donovan, handed the mike back. Justin watched in frustration—he wanted so badly to be the one comforting her.

Mercedes spoke next, without the mike. Holding her candle in one hand, she squeezed Steve's hand with the other and said, "I just want to tell you guys to look out for each other. Stick with a friend when you go out. I don't want to go to another one of these vigils. Diamond, wherever you are, you know you're my girl. Come back, you hear? Come back."

Justin walked up and took the microphone next. "I just wanna say to Mr. and Mrs. Landers, and Shasta, that it's gonna be okay. Seriously. I just know it. Diamond is like her name—bright but tough. She will be back, and soon."

At least two dozen students and teachers made comments, many of them, like Justin, sharing words of encouragement to Diamond's family. In spite of the nasty drizzle, nobody seemed to want to leave.

Mrs. Gennari took the mike once more. "As we leave this place, I want you all to think of the power of these candles we see flickering here tonight. Diamond is missing. But the lights I see around me give me hope."

She paused and unfolded a sheet of notebook paper. "I'd like to read something—something written by Diamond last year, for a language arts research project that she did on missing children," she said. "Her mother found it in Diamond's desk drawer and has given us permission to read it. I've only changed the very first and very last lines."

Justin looked up sharply.

Mrs. Gennari said, "Please hold up your candles, my friends." She lifted her own arm, and her candle burned brightly. She cleared her throat and began.

> *"This candle is Diamond, who's missing tonight*
> *This candle is Lisa and Ken*
> *This candle is all those who can't find the light*
> *This candle is love deep within.*
>
> *This candle is Shayla, who's lovely and thin*
> *And Kelly, who lived on the phone*
> *It's Mona and Alex and Buddy and Kim,*
> *Whose parents have hope made of stone.*
>
> *This candle is searchers who look for the lost*
> *Officers and friends with no fears*
> *Who never get glory or count up the cost*
> *As they seek to erase all the tears.*
>
> *This candle is dancers, musicians, and scribes*
> *Who ease all our pain with their art*
> *It's dreamers and poets and rappers with vibes*
> *Who help us to unbreak our hearts.*
>
> *If the glow from one candle can brighten the night*
> *The glow of one thousand can blind.*
> *And when Diamond comes home, she'll feel this great light*
> *And know how our love for her shines. "*

Justin thought the poem was pretty weak, but the message was strong. *It's kinda creepy that she wrote it over a year ago,* he thought.

"Keep Diamond and all missing children in your hearts and prayers tonight," Mrs. Gennari said as the vigil ended. "Blow out your candles and leave them in the boxes provided. Go home with your families and treasure each other." With that, she dismissed them all.

But as the flickering lights sputtered out in tiny puffs of smoke, Justin felt a cold chill. It was too much like a hundred small deaths happening all at once.

23

MERCEDES, *Sunday, April 14   10 p.m.*

"The night was peppered with stars."

—from *Peter Pan*

Mercedes and Steve huddled together in Steve's unheated Buick. They'd parked the car in front of the house, and Mercedes had noticed her mother peek out of her bedroom window at least twice in the last fifteen minutes.

The car had once been a sleek, metallic green, but years of sun and snow, of dents and dings, had dulled it to a heap of metal the color of cabbage. The back bumper was held on with duct tape, and a long, wobbling crack snaked across the front windshield.

"Your car, is, without a doubt, the ugliest vehicle in the universe," she said, scooting closer to Steve.

"Yep, that it is," he replied, putting his arm around her. "But you know you love it."

"Only because *you* do."

"I paid for it all by myself," he said proudly.

"Couldn't have been hard to come up with ten dollars and thirty-nine cents," she teased.

"It's got personality!" he said.

"My dad's car starts with a push of a button. He doesn't even need a key."

"Well, my car starts with a push too—especially in the middle of winter."

They both laughed.

"Can you believe that somebody once pulled out of a car dealership and drove it home, all proud?" Mercedes said as she rubbed a finger over the worn leather seats.

"It was shiny and gleaming."

"Both headlights and both taillights worked."

"The horn honked."

"The blinkers blinked."

"All four windows rolled down."

"The finest piece of automotive excellence that 1989 had to offer."

"My mother taught me to respect senior citizens," she said with a laugh, "so I'm being nice to Miss Ethyl."

"If my honey car thinks you don't love her, she'll spit

oil on your new jeans and ooze rust on your best jacket," Steve warned.

"I think she's already done that," Mercedes said. "She was trying to let me know she was boss."

"Ethyl may be an eyesore, but she gets me over here to see you, and that's all that counts," he whispered into Mercedes' ear.

Mercedes snuggled into Steve's embrace. "The vigil tonight was nice, in a weird way. Do you think it did any good?"

"I don't know—I guess it helped," Steve replied, "because we needed to come together and worry about her all in one place at the same time. And it had to have helped her parents—to know so many people cared."

"Do you think Diamond knows? How many people care, I mean?" Mercedes asked, hope in her voice.

"She's gotta know people are worried about her and searching for her," Steve assured her.

"I sure hope so," Mercedes said with a sigh.

"Look, it gave all of us a feeling of togetherness. Sometimes that's all you can do when you're feeling sad and messed up."

"When did you get so wise?" Mercedes teased. "Anyway, I know you always make *me* feel better." She grabbed his hand and squeezed it.

"Hey, I'm just as confused and scared as everybody else," Steve admitted. "What if it was *you* who was missing? I'd be going crazy round 'bout now."

"Really?"

"You even have to ask?" He hugged her close.

"Uh, Steve," Mercedes said in a tiny voice.

"What's up?"

"It's still raining, and Miss Ethyl's hole-spattered roof is leaking all over my head." Mercedes moved Steve's hand to the soaked top of her hoodie.

"Hey, you found the one disadvantage of my one-of-a-kind air-conditioning system!" Steve said. "Look at it this way—I have a built-in sprinkler!" They both laughed. "But I better get you inside. I don't want my car to be the reason you catch pneumonia."

He kissed her gently, pulled open the squeaky door, and they both scrambled to her front porch. At her front door, he kissed her once more, then he trotted back to the raggedy car.

It started up with a cough and a sputter, but the motor finally turned over. Steve roared down the street, waving his arm until he turned the corner and Mercedes could no longer see him.

24

DIAMOND, *Sunday, April 14   10 p.m.*

"The goals are at each end of the rainbow."
—from *Peter Pan*

Diamond startled awake and nearly fell from the chair when she heard the door being unlocked. She braced herself, then, just as Thane walked in, she bolted across the floor to the opening. He caught her easily with one hand.

"*Don't* make me tie you up again," he hissed. He pushed her onto the bed.

Diamond scrambled back up. "Please let me go home.

I promise I won't tell anybody anything. I'll . . . I'll tell people I ran away because I had a fight with my mother. No one will ever know what happened. I swear! Just let me go. Please."

"Not a chance. You were a *big* hit on the Internet last night." He nodded up and down with a smug smile. "A *big* hit."

"Internet?" Diamond whispered, stepping backward.

"Of course. People pay big money to watch you strut your stuff."

Diamond gagged. "No—no. Oh God, no. People *watched*? Oh, God. Oh, God." She looked up at him through welling eyes. "How can you do this? You have to know this is wrong."

"Feels right to me!" Thane replied cheerfully. He pulled a Big Mac from one jacket pocket and a bottle of water from another. "Here, I brought you dinner. Eat well. You'll need your strength tonight." He threw them on the bed and left.

As soon as he'd locked the door behind him, Diamond burst into tears once more. She cried until her breath came in ragged hiccups. The inside of her mouth felt dry and parched.

People were watching? *Watching?* What was she going to do? What was she going to do? She peered up at the unreachable window. She tried the door again, banging on it with her fists, scratching at the edges until her fingers bled. Nothing.

She lay back down at the bottom of the bed and curled in a ball, wanting to die. But she was *so* thirsty.

And hungry, she realized. She hated herself for eating, but she gobbled the cold, soggy sandwich and drank the water anyway.

The dizziness and fogginess came back almost immediately. *Oh, no! Stoopid. Stoopid. I shoulda known. Shoulda, shoulda . . .* But she could no longer think clearly. The drugs were clogging her brain once more.

Diamond was only vaguely aware of Thane when he returned. She blinked at the bright studio lights. She winced as he tied her arms to the bed, but she couldn't get command of her muscles to fight back. She tried to struggle, but she was too weak. She was aware of deep bass laughter. A male voice she did not recognize. The cloying, overpowering cologne of a tall, thin stranger who hovered near the bed. Her last clear image was of his face. He was leering at her. He was licking his lips.

After that, everything was a painful blur.

25

JUSTIN, *Monday, April 15   5 p.m.*

"Such a deliciously creepy song it was . . ."
—from *Peter Pan*

The mood at the studio on Monday evening was grim. Students whispered nervously in small groups. No one watched television in the café. No one bought snacks. No one danced.

Freakin' eerie, Justin thought. Everyone at school had talked of nothing else all day, except where was Diamond Landers? What could have happened to her?

And still the rain poured down. Justin couldn't

remember the last time he'd seen sunlight.

He forced himself to begin warm-ups in his favorite corner of the largest dance room. Two girls whispered frantically in the opposite corner. Another girl did a series of deep knee bends over and over and over. Two others sat with heads bowed, not speaking to anyone. He felt the same uncertainty.

After dismissing the five- and six-year-olds from their class, Miss Ginger hurried into the room. "Let's circle up, guys," she said warmly. "We need to talk."

Justin managed to position himself between Layla and Mercedes. Layla didn't seem to notice. Or care, for that matter.

"Have you heard anything, Miss Ginger?" Zizi asked, her eyes bright. "Have the police given you any updates?"

"You watch too much TV," Mercedes told her.

"You can learn a lot from reruns of *Law and Order*," Zizi said, glaring at her.

"Doubt it," Layla retorted, rolling her eyes.

"Well, I have personally passed out five hundred of the flyers from the vigil and nailed at least a hundred to telephone poles," Zizi asserted.

"Hey, that's great," Layla said, her face softening. "That's really great."

Zizi nodded, then turned to Miss Ginger and, checking out her teacher's outfit—a sleek black leotard and top, a red warm-up, and soft red dance boots—she nodded approvingly and said, "If there's ever a contest for best-dressed dance teacher, Miss Ginger would win it for sure!"

"This isn't about me," Miss Ginger said with a smile. "We need to talk about Diamond."

"Is there any news?" Justin asked.

"Just a little."

The room went instantly quiet.

"I spoke to Diamond's mother, and the police were able to get some good footage from the mall security tapes."

Everyone asked the same question at once. "What did they see?"

"Her mom told me it shows Diamond talking to a man about forty years old, tall and good-looking. It shows her texting something—her message to you, Mercedes, they assume. And then they see her walking out with the man. She is smiling. So is the man. The footage stops when she gets into his car—a dark sedan."

"Did they get the license plates?" Justin asked.

"No. I think she said the perpetrator had covered them up somehow. But his picture is being blasted all over the news media, along with Diamond's yearbook photo."

"She hates that picture," Mercedes said, shaking her head.

"If it's the picture that finds her, it's the best one ever taken. Someone will surely call. Somebody has to know this monster!" Miss Ginger was inhaling and exhaling slowly—Justin could tell she was trying to calm herself down.

His stomach began to contract into a knot. If the man covered his license plates, there was no way he was taking

Diamond to a movie audition. No way. Justin stood up and began pacing. This was bad. Really bad.

"Do you think she's scared?" Tara asked, scooting closer to her twin.

"I'm sure she is," Miss Ginger replied. "But she's very brave and awfully smart, and I'm sure she's looking out for herself."

"Miss Ginger?" Tina asked in a small voice.

"Yes, Tina?"

Tina picked at a thread on her ballet slippers. "You don't think she's, uh, she's, uh, hurt or something, do you?"

"I'll be honest with you—I really don't know. But I'm praying with all my being that she is safe and will find her way home, and back to us as well."

Jillian shook her head. "This kind of stuff is supposed to happen to strangers, not somebody we know."

"Do you think anyone will call?" Tina asked.

"The mall is a big place, and lots of people were there when the incident occurred," Miss Ginger replied. "So there's a chance, right?"

Justin pulled up from a stretch. "Folks sometimes don't like to get involved," he said.

Jillian pulled the scrunchie off her ponytail, shook her hair, then put the scrunchie back. She did that several times, pacing the floor. Finally she said, "What I can't believe is that she got in a car with a total stranger! That's just plain dumb!"

Zizi threw her arms up. "I woulda done it. Gone with the dude. Fastened his seat belt. Bought him lunch.

Helped him drive. I admit it. I'm the dumbest bunny in the garden."

That caused a small ripple of smiles.

"I think I mighta gone with the man if I thought I could be in a movie," Tara admitted.

"Me too," said her twin, "but only if my sister could go with me."

"So I'd be making *two* flyers instead of one!" Zizi groaned.

"I didn't think about that," said Tina.

"This is crazy!" Jillian continued. "An offer to be in a movie is just too good to be true! Dumb! Dumb! Dumb!" She pounded her fist on the floor.

"Don't you *dare* call Diamond dumb!" Mercedes lashed out. "You've never done anything you wished you hadn't, Miss Perfect?"

Jillian looked surprised, then changed her tone. "I'm sorry. I didn't mean that. Sure, I've done lots of stupid stuff. I'm just so freaked!"

"I feel you," Justin admitted.

Lil Bit tore at a hole in her tights. "The thing is, there's just no way Diamond would have run away. No freakin' way. And why would she want to? It makes no sense."

"I know!" Layla chimed in. "She's got parents like out of a storybook. Her mom is a teacher; her dad is lawyer. They go to places like Disney World every summer. She's crazy about her folks and her little sister. Who'd run away from that?"

Jillian flexed her toes back and forth, then said

carefully, "Sometimes what you see on the outside is not the real deal."

Layla shook her head vehemently. "No. It is—at least for Diamond." She paused, then, after a moment, added, "I wouldn't have gone with him."

"Why not?" Justin asked.

"Donny would hate me being a movie star," she admitted.

"So your decision wouldn't be based on danger, but on Donovan?" Justin asked. He couldn't believe what she was saying.

"Not that it's any of your business, but what does it matter? I'd be safe either way." She scooted away from Justin and crossed her arms across her chest.

Shoot! Now he'd blown it! "I'm not judgin'," he said quickly, trying to calm her down. "We're just having a conversation here."

"Guys! Guys!" Miss Ginger said gently. "The anxiety in this room feels like a rubber band about to snap. Let's do some stretches, then you can say or ask anything that's in your heart."

"Anything?" Elizabeth asked, her eyes wide. "There's some stuff I'm scared to ask out loud."

"Anything. We're family here," Miss Ginger assured her.

She chose the song "Tender Shepherd" from the original, Mary Martin version of *Peter Pan*. She turned it up just a bit, then said in a soft, soothing voice, "Now, each of you, bend forward, reach past your toes on your right leg. Good. Now stretch. Slowly. Once again. Good. Now the left leg. Once again. Good. Now, both arms up.

Stretch. Reach for the ceiling. Right arm. Reach. Circle it. Again. Left arm. Reach. Circle it. Again."

The song, a delicate lullaby of intertwined children's voices, pipes, and violas, trilled with tones of hope and safety and comfort.

As the dancers rolled on their backs, stretched their hips, their legs and arms, and their torsos, they all started relaxing. Miss Ginger switched the song to Whitney Houston's "Where Do Broken Hearts Go?" as she pumped up the intensity of the workout.

The words made Justin's breath catch in his throat as he moved to the music. *"Where do broken hearts go/Can they find their way home . . ."*

When the workout was over, Miss Ginger turned the music down low again and let everyone catch their breaths.

"I know this is not what we usually do in class, but I'm not in the mood for leaping and cavorting right now, and I know you aren't either."

"Thanks for the stretches, Miss G.," Jillian said. "We needed that and didn't even know it."

"I feel a little better," Mercedes admitted. "I haven't slept much the last couple of nights."

"Me neither," Layla said.

"Are we still gonna do *Peter Pan*, Miss Ginger?" Zizi asked.

"Yes, we certainly are," Miss Ginger replied.

"I'm really excited about being the crocodile and Nana the dog," Zizi said, giving a convincing growl.

"Why?" asked Justin, glad Zizi had changed the subject to a lighter tone.

"Well, duh! It's character acting! Anybody can do a stupid lyrical solo, but it takes skills to convince people you've got a tick-tocking clock in your belly. Can you cue up the second song, Miss Ginger?" Zizi asked, passing her iPod to her teacher. "I've been working on my piece already!"

Miss Ginger nodded, scrolled through the iPod, and pushed PLAY. The song "Tick Tock" from the movie *Sherlock Holmes: A Game of Shadows* exploded from the speakers. The music was mysterious and dramatic, with the slightest ticking rhythm pattering in syncopation in the background. Zizi seemed to exult in the deep bass notes, the minor key, twisting her body across the floor in time with the power of the music. She crawled on her belly. She stretched her arms and legs as if she really were a swimming crocodile, a beast on the hunt. Justin was impressed.

When the song ended, with drums, cellos, and that subtle ticking, the whole class gave Zizi a round of applause.

"What a great piece of improv work!" Miss Ginger exclaimed. "We'll have to work that into the show."

Zizi stood up and bowed deeply. "Choreography by ZZC! That's my stage name," she explained, grinning. But then she grew serious. "I'm . . ." Her voice broke. She tried again. "It's not right that Diamond's not here. So I'm . . . I'm dedicating my dance to Diamond." She sat down, flushed and wobbly.

Mercedes raised her hand. "May I, too, Miss Ginger?" she asked softly. "Sometimes that's the only way I can get my feelings out—I gotta dance!"

"Why, of course! In fact"—Miss Ginger looked to each of her students—"anyone who feels like it, this is your chance."

As the whole class moved to the mirror-covered wall and sat down, Justin was bummed to see that Layla had chosen to sit as far away from him as possible. Yep, he'd totally blown it.

Mercedes went first. She chose "Everybody Hurts" by Avril Lavigne and let it play for a few bars before she began. She untied her hair and let it swing and fling as her arms and legs matched the wildness of it. Justin could feel her fear and frustration more palpably than anything she could have put into words. The song embraced them all as she danced.

She leaped and pranced and swept across the floor. Justin imagined Avril's words echoed everyone's thoughts. *"So many questions/So much on my mind/So many answers I can't find . . ."* When Mercedes finished her dance, she was sweating and weeping.

No one clapped. Respectful silence was all that was needed.

Miss Ginger ran to her and hugged her tightly. "And it *will* be okay. I just know it will."

"Thanks," Mercedes said breathlessly. "That felt great!"

Miss Ginger escorted Mercedes back to her place at the wall. "Good. You needed that."

Tara and Tina raised their hands next. "Can we dance together, Miss G.?"

"Don't you always?" Miss Ginger said with a grin.

The twins grinned back and chose "Mirror" by Monica for their piece. As the group listened to the words, *"When I look at myself in the mirror . . . I'll never have to search again . . . ,"* the twins danced as if each were looking at a mirror image of herself. Their movements were poised, precise, and identical. They lowered their heads and lifted their left arms upward at exactly the same time and touched palms. Then they extended their right arms, touched palms again, and twisted in unison to the rhythm of the piece. They sprung into the air, legs leaping and landing at the exact same time. They continued the dance, bouncing and twirling across the floor, each one's movements mirroring the other's from start to finish. Justin was amazed—he'd never seen them dance like that before.

The class clapped wildly when the twins finished. They bowed together and sat down.

"I wish Diamond could see this," Zizi said. "She'd feel so good knowing what we were doing."

"Can I go next?" Jillian asked.

"Are you going to do your solo from *The Nutcracker*?" Miss Ginger asked. Jillian's snow queen solo was legendary. Graceful and glorious, it was her signature piece. She always won high golds doing it at competitions, gliding regally across the stage.

"No, not today. I just want Diamond to know we care about her and that she's got friends. Would you put on Cris Williamson's 'Sister,' please?"

Miss Ginger nodded and cued up the song on the iPod. Moving smoothly to the easy rhythms, Jillian's dance was a series of glissades and piqué turns and abstract contemporary moves that required balance and extreme flexibility. As the melody floated from the speakers, the singer's clear, plaintive voice echoed with the clarity of a crystal bell. Jillian made the words come alive. *"And you can count on me to share the load . . . Lean on me, I am your sister/Believe on me, I am your friend . . ."*

She ended with a deep bow. Everyone exploded in applause.

Each student who chose to dance picked a piece that fit their personality and showed their fear or worry or Diamond's desperation. Justin had to admit the whole experience was powerfully moving.

When almost everyone else had danced, Justin raised his hand. "Miss Ginger, can I do a pas de deux, please?"

"Sure. Who would you like to partner with?"

Justin's heart thudded. But he managed to say her name without stuttering or acting like a seventh-grader. "Layla. If she agrees, of course."

Layla looked at him with steely eyes, but she rose without complaint and took his outstretched hand. He asked Miss Ginger to start the song—Katy Perry's "Firework." They had performed to this music for a competition a year ago, and although he was sure Layla had forgotten all about it, he remembered every second.

He hoped she was paying attention to the lyrics—the song seemed to be just what she needed to hear. *"'Cause there's a spark in you . . . You don't have to feel like a waste of space . . ."*

He led her gently through the lifts and turns as the music flowed over both of them, and he could feel her begin to relax as the song progressed. He knew that even though she might not like him much, she loved this music, and she loved the movement of this dance.

The song ended with a gentle glide and a small turn, which left them facing each other. He smiled at her and, amazingly, she allowed him a small smile in return. He held her hand while they took their bows, hating the moment when he had to release her and return to his seat on the floor.

"That was simply lovely," Miss Ginger said. "I'm so glad you started this, Zizi. We couldn't have paid for a better therapy session. That's a wrap for this evening. I want you all to go home and get a good night's sleep and say a prayer for Diamond before you drift off."

As they left the studio, Miss Ginger caught Justin's arm. "That pas de deux was some of the best dancing you and Layla have ever done. It was almost magical."

Justin felt his face go hot. "Thanks. We were really in sync for a minute."

"Perhaps I should pair the two of you for a recital piece. Maybe even for summer competitions, if you'd like to do that."

"It's cool with me. Ask Layla." It took all Justin's composure to stop himself from leaping across the floor. Miss Ginger winked at him, and Justin could tell she completely understood.

By the time he got his gear together, he saw Layla just leaving the studio. She was walking out to the parking lot, heading, he knew, toward Donovan's Escalade.

26

LAYLA, *Monday, April 15   8:30 p.m.*

"Are all the children chained, so that they cannot fly away?"
—from *Peter Pan*

"I saw you dancing with him. I watched through the window."

"I don't even get a 'Hey, what's up? How've you been?' before you start jumping all up in my business?"

"You *are* my business. And I watched every minute of that dance. He had his freakin' hands all over you and you were *liking* it!"

Not again! Layla sighed. "What I like is dancing. I don't care who my partner is."

"But I do. I saw him tryin' to feel you up."

"He was not! He has to hold on to me to lift me and to make sure I don't fall."

"You're done dancing with him. *Done!* I mean it."

"Donny, he's the only guy in our class. The other male dancers are just kids—eleven and twelve. So Justin has to dance with every girl in our class, including me. There's no way around it!" How could he not get this, she wondered in frustration.

Donovan jerked the car to the side of the road and slammed on the brake. The fury on his face made Layla draw back against the door. He ever so gently put a hand up to her neck and just as gently began to squeeze. Layla froze. Donovan smiled, a smile that in any other circumstance would be described as sweet, and said, "Then maybe it's time you quit dancing."

"Quit?" She tried to jerk away from him. "You trippin'!"

He squeezed harder.

"Donny! You're hurting me!" she said, trying to squirm from his grip.

"I think you need to spend more time with me," he hissed.

She caught his hands in her own and tried to release the pressure. She had to calm him down. "But we're together every day at school and every day after dance class. What more could you want?"

"More! You go to those stupid classes every freakin' day. For hours. I'm sick of it!" He squeezed harder still.

"But I can't quit dancing," she wheezed out, clawing at his hand.

"I thought you loved me." He increased the pressure.

Layla's mind reeled—he was going to kill her if he didn't stop. She could barely speak. "Please. You. Are. Hurting. Me. Stop! Stop!"

He squeezed even harder. "Then you got some decisions to make."

She felt dizzy. Her words gurgled. "You. Know. I. Love. You. Please. Let. Go." She could tell she was about to black out.

He released his hand. Layla slumped in relief against the door, inhaling and exhaling sharply. She rolled down the window, gulping the damp air.

A few moments later, as if nothing had happened, he said, "You want to stop and get a burger?"

Still drawing in huge gulps of air, Layla nodded mutely as Donovan put the car in drive and roared into the rain-drenched night.

27

DIAMOND, *Tuesday, April 16   9 a.m.*

"Perhaps mother is in half mourning by this time."
—from *Peter Pan*

Thane unlocked the door and entered with Diamond's breakfast and a change of clothes. He set the food on the bed. "I hope you slept well," he said cheerfully. "The last few nights have been simply glorious. It never occurred to me how much more . . . ah, flexible . . . dancers could be."

Diamond was not going to give him the satisfaction of a response. She covered her head with her arms.

"Shower up, sweetie. I've got a surprise for you today."

"What? More drugs? You drugged me again," she accused him as he led her into the bathroom.

"I find it makes things easier for everyone involved," he explained.

"When are you going to let me go home?"

"Soon. I promise. Soon." He turned on the shower, placed her fresh clothes on the toilet, and left.

Diamond let the hot water pound at her battered body. She didn't want to look at the places where the bruises were. She didn't want to give up, but her hopes were dimming.

She left the bathroom and got dressed. He always brought her really nice clothes—things she would have chosen, and brand-new every day. What was up with that? Once again, he had changed the sheets. Today they were soft pink. Sitting gingerly in the chair, she forced herself to choke down the breakfast of juice and a couple of doughnuts. She flung the stupid rose into the corner.

She looked, just as she looked a dozen times a day, up at the inaccessible window. She wondered if there was any way she could jump on the bed hard enough to bounce up there, and then thought to herself she was definitely losing it—it was fifteen feet up! She could barely make out bullet-gray skies and steady rain.

For some reason this time, snippets of songs she'd danced to wove their way through her mind. "Bluebird" by Sara Bareilles, who sang of wings torn and rusted, and of flying away. "Beautiful Flower" by India.Arie, which she'd always liked because the song was about power and fire and diamonds. But even though she knew she had no chance to fly away just yet, Diamond decided to focus on that power. To keep herself sane, she decided to concentrate on a way to escape.

She found energy in thinking about the studio, which always felt comfortable, like a favorite sweatshirt. The smell of popcorn from the microwave in the café, the swirling strains of thousands of songs, the glaring reality of the mirrors that covered each wall. Miss Ginger's voice, demanding and gentle at the same time. The sound of fifteen pairs of tap shoes on the wooden floor. Sweat— honest, exhilarating sweat after a great class.

She thought about her friends all the time. To fill the silence of the long hours of the day, she made up little conversations with them in her head.

To Mercedes: "Girl, I have landed in the hotel of Hell. I'd give anything to spend a day with you in Eden Park, down by the river, just talkin' trash and sendin' texts."

To Justin: "I hope you've told Layla how you feel, you big doofus. You know where they get the word *lovely*? From love. Real love. Not the ugly stuff. I'd kill for some lovely right about now. You've got it at your fingertips."

To Layla: "I'm glad you got the part of Wendy in *Peter Pan*. Dance like the star you are, girlfriend. Dance away from that turd you're hooked up with."

To her parents: "Mommy? Daddy? Remember when I used to call you that? Can I be your little girl again? I'm gettin' out of this place somehow, and I'm comin' home."

Hours went by, then Thane unlocked the door. He

was smiling as usual, this time carrying a small box in his hand. Bella the dog trotted beside him. "I want to keep you as happy as possible," he said, holding out one hand.

She glared at him. "Then let me go home."

"Unfortunately, that's not possible right yet, but I did bring you something to help pass the time." He handed her the box.

Diamond looked at it suspiciously. "I don't want anything from you."

"I think you'll be pleased. Open it." Thane's cheerfulness made her skin crawl.

Grudgingly, Diamond opened the purple foil-wrapped package. Inside was a brand-new iPod—the latest model, with tiny earbuds to go with it.

"Why?" she asked him dully.

"Just call it a reward for good behavior."

"I don't want it." She threw it on the floor.

"Now, now. I took the time to download every possible song that teenagers might like, plus all the songs you had on your cell phone."

Diamond looked up sharply. "You have my cell phone?"

"Of course. I plugged it in and charged it. You've had *lots* of calls lately. I wonder what *that's* all about." He gave a humorless smirk.

"Can't the police trace my location through my cell phone?" she asked hopefully.

"You've been watching too many crime shows," he said, his eyes narrowing. "That only happens on TV. Now, you can leave the player on the floor, or you can fill your day with music. It's up to you."

He left the room, locking the door with a solid *click*.

Diamond sat stunned for a moment. People had been calling her, looking for her! But what were they thinking? Did they think she'd run away? Oh God, she couldn't stand it. She paced the room and nearly stepped on the music player on the floor. She stared at it with hatred, but she couldn't stand the dense, enveloping silence of the room that held her prisoner.

She picked it up, turned it on, and pressed the play arrow. She could barely stand that Thane was right. But when she found her dance pieces, she felt her body relax as she listened.

She cued up "Black Butterfly" by Deniece Williams. The song was about faith and survival, about struggling and never giving up, about being proud and beautiful. Diamond looked around at the despised room, thinking ruefully that she felt neither the pride nor the beauty that the song celebrated. But she played the song over and over and over, until a pebble of determination began to take shape. Somehow, some way, someday she was going to get out of here. She was *not* going to let Thane crush her.

Diamond closed her eyes and let herself be swept away on a cushion of music. She dozed. She dreamed of dancing.

"Black butterfly/Set the skies on fire/Rise up even higher so the wind can catch your wings . . ."

28

LAYLA, *Tuesday, April 16   9–11 a.m.*

"Steadily the waters rose till they were nibbling at his feet."
—from *Peter Pan*

Layla decided to skip school on Tuesday. She didn't call or text Donny or any of her friends. She knew if there'd been news about Diamond, one of the girls would have told her.

"You're gonna be late, Layla," her mother said, tapping on her bedroom door.

"I've got a cold, Mom. I'm gonna sleep in, all right?" Layla hoped her mother wouldn't check her temperature.

"Okay, sweetie. I've got to do a double shift today. Think you'll make it to dance class?"

"Yeah. I hope so, if I feel better."

"Feel better, honey. See you tonight."

"Thanks, Mom." Layla frowned. Her mom still hadn't said anything about her dad being released, and Layla still hadn't told her that she knew. She guessed they'd play this game until he walked through the door. But the truth was, she was itching with excitement.

The nonstop rain made everything feel so damp and chilly. So she made herself get up, take a hot shower, and finally look at herself in the mirror. She stepped backward in shock—her neck was darkened and bluish. She touched the bruises gently and winced. How could Donny have done this to her? She tried to remember how great it was when they'd first started going out, and when it all started to unravel. It had been so gradual— the love, the anger, and the fear all mixed up like a really bad abstract painting.

The girl looking back at her in the mirror looked pretty unhappy. Layla made a face at herself. She wished she knew how to figure out this love stuff. He loved her, right? He had to—otherwise he wouldn't have gotten so upset. But still . . . She shook her head in confusion.

She dug down in her bottom dresser drawer until she found a turtleneck. Yanking it on, she checked the mirror. Good. The red shirt covered up most of the bruises. She found some jeans, pulled on her favorite fuzzy slippers, and curled up on the sofa. The house smelled vaguely of the cookies her mother had baked last night for her latest gentleman friend, who'd come over to watch a movie after their date.

Layla didn't turn the TV on. She didn't cry. She just sat there, thinking, feeling crazy scared of losing Donny, of giving up dance—dance was the one thing that made her completely happy. She tried to imagine herself in Donny's place—she *did* spend a lot of time at the studio, much more time than with him. No wonder it ticked him off. And she sure got jealous when *she* thought about Magnificent Jones sliding around *him*—she'd be furious if she knew he was touching Mag. And yet he had to watch Justin have his hands on her every day.

So she got it: he was jealous. That was why he'd acted like such a jerk last night. It made sense in a weird sort of way.

She rocked back and forth, thinking. Maybe she could just stop dance for a few weeks until he cooled down. But her mother worked double shifts to pay for the lessons—she'd be really pissed if she quit. And then there was the lead in *Peter Pan*. Man, this was hard! But to lose Donny? She tried so hard to make him happy—she was a good girlfriend. She didn't know how she'd make it without him. She couldn't lose him—she just couldn't. Her thoughts spun with confusion.

When her phone beeped, she grabbed it with relief. It was Mercedes.

where r u?

hme. Sick.

u shld b here

164

y

donny

wym

he w mag. like i tld u.

su! mag? why? i dnt gt it.

cause mag is hot.

im not?

not like tht. u 2 hve a fight?

not xactly.

well, hes all up in hr face 2day.

wat shld i do?

let her have him.

i cant!

y

u can't c wat i c.

i c him w mag 2day.

i no wat 2 do. got this.

g2g. bell abt 2 ring. l8tr.

Layla felt sick to her stomach. He was with Mag. For real—she knew it. Mercedes wouldn't have texted otherwise. How could he *do* this to her? The thought of Donny with Mag made her want to throw up. She imagined him touching her, kissing her, whispering in her ear. Mag would laugh that deep and throaty laugh of hers and would never say no to anything Donny asked for.

She fired off several texts to him, but he did not respond.

So she threw on a jacket and her Uggs, locked the front door, and hurried out into the damp morning.

Waiting impatiently for the bus, she tried to keep visions of Donovan and Magnificent out of her head. *Why is he doing this?* she asked herself again and again as she scrunched herself into a seat next to a very large woman.

But she knew the answer. And she knew what Donny wanted her to do. She got off the bus in front of the dance studio. Miss Ginger's VW Beetle sat in the parking lot. Layla sighed with relief as she knocked on the studio door.

"Well, this is a surprise," Miss Ginger said, unlocking the door. "You came to help me empty trash and clean bathrooms?"

"Not exactly," Layla replied.

"I'm not going to even ask why you're not in school. I guess you have a really good reason."

"I skipped."

"Tell me something I don't know."

"I need to talk to somebody."

"You know I'm always here for you kids. What's up? You worried about Diamond? I sure am."

"What I don't understand is why she'd do something we've all been warned about since we were kids! Never talk to strangers. Even her little sister knows that." Layla paced the freshly cleaned dance floor.

"You want to take those boots off?" Miss Ginger said, nodding toward the mop.

"Oh, my bad," Layla said, pulling them off. She grabbed the mop and cleared the wet tracks she'd made.

"So, is this day off from school because Diamond is missing?" Miss Ginger asked carefully.

Layla sank down in one of the many beanbag chairs that lined the walls of the dance room. "This is gonna sound weird: I'm not missing like Diamond is, but it's like sometimes I feel like I'm not really here, you know?"

"What do you mean?"

"Never mind. I'm just really down today." Layla glanced out the window. "Why won't it stop raining?"

Miss Ginger waited.

"You got anything to eat here?" Layla blurted out.

Miss Ginger put her hands on her hips. "I know you didn't skip school to feast on granola bars from the vending machine. What's really on your mind, Layla? You know I'm strict on grades and such. I can't have one of my best dancers running the streets on a school day."

Layla hesitated. "Do you really think I'm a good dancer?"

"Absolutely. As I said, one of the best I have. You're still learning, but I've seen so much growth in you this year."

"Really?"

"I wouldn't lie to you. Why do you think you got the part of Wendy?"

Layla dipped her head. "I thought maybe you just felt sorry for me."

"Have I *ever* assigned a part to anyone out of sympathy? You don't give yourself the credit you deserve." Miss Ginger looked downright huffy.

"It's just that, well, have you ever looked in the mirror and felt ugly? Fat? I know that must be how I look when I dance."

"Actually, when you dance you are at your most beautiful. Seriously."

"I'm getting fat."

"Who told you that? Not your mirror. You are lithe and lovely—the perfect size for a healthy dancer."

Layla groaned. "*Healthy* is a code word that grown-ups use for *fat*."

"Not true. You know me better than that. You've been dancing with me since you were six years old. And you know I'm honest with my assessments."

"I was happy when I was six." Layla hesitated. "My dad was still around then."

"You must really miss him."

"More than you know."

"He sure was one big fan of your dancing!"

"Yeah. I guess he still is. I send him pictures from all our recitals and shows. He tells me they keep him going."

"I'm sure they do. Doesn't it help when you visit him?" Miss Ginger asked.

Layla looked down. "He got sent to a place way upstate. Mom goes to see him about once a year. But she always refuses to take me—says it isn't a proper place for a child."

Miss Ginger placed her hand on her heart. "Oh, I had no idea!"

"Yeah. It sucks. But guess what?"

"What, hon?"

"Well, Mom never tells me anything about his release hearings, but I'm pretty sure he's getting out this week."

"This week? Really?"

"I found a letter in the kitchen drawer. It doesn't specify exactly what day, but it says this week."

"I'd say that's the best news I've heard in a long time," Miss Ginger said, slapping her leg.

"Me too." Layla took a breath. "But I've changed a lot since I was ten. What if . . . what if he remembers me one way, and I'm not that way anymore? What if he doesn't like the way I am now?"

"Layla, he's your father. He adores you. You know that."

"I guess. But it's still, I don't know, strange to think about him being home again after all this time. He's probably different too."

"How has your mom dealt with your dad's absence?"

"Working too hard. Playing too hard. She never has two minutes for me."

"But she also believes in you, Layla. I know she struggles to make your dance fees, but she's never missed a payment."

Layla sighed. "Yeah, I know. So maybe I should make it easier on her."

"How's that?"

"Maybe I should quit dancing for a while," Layla said in a rush. She searched Miss Ginger's face for her reaction.

Miss Ginger paused. "You know you always have that option, Layla, but I'd like for you to think it through."

"I've already thought about it! I just gotta quit!" And at this, Layla burst into tears.

Miss Ginger let her cry, then handed her a clean dust-cloth. "Wipe your eyes, then spray some Windex on the mirrors for me."

Layla sniffed, got herself together, then filled the

mirror with the blue spray. She sprayed on so much she could no longer see herself. "What good is this gonna do?" she asked glumly.

Miss Ginger didn't answer right away. Finally she asked, "What's this about for real, Layla? It's not really your mom, is it? Is this about Diamond?"

Layla continued to wipe and spray, spray and wipe. "No," she admitted in a small voice.

Miss Ginger began to clean the mirror from the other end. For a while there were only the sounds of the spray gushing out of the bottle and the squeak of a cloth on the glass.

"Have you ever been in love, Miss Ginger?" Layla finally asked.

Miss Ginger smiled. "Yes, I have. It's the most glorious, horrible, wonderful, confusing feeling in the world."

Layla scrubbed furiously at a fingerprint on the mirror. "So how come I just got the horrible part of it?"

Miss Ginger set down her spray bottle. "You talking about Donovan?"

"Yeah."

"Do you love him?"

"I think so. I love making him happy. His smile gives me the shivers."

"You know, Layla, it's nice to want to give joy to the people you care about. But what does *he* do to make *you* feel good about yourself?"

"He picks me up every day after class. He waits for me without complaining when I'm late—well, most of the time."

"I'd do the same for a pet puppy."

"He takes me for burgers and pizza. He buys me shoes."

"Anything else?"

"He looks so good, and his car is so nice, and he lets everybody at school know we're together."

"Uh-huh."

"He's got *my name* tattooed on his arm," Layla said proudly.

"You still haven't told me how he makes *you* happy. I don't see you smiling much these days. You've seemed stressed and skittish. And what's up with the marks on your neck and your arm?"

Layla quickly tugged up her turtleneck. "I, uh, slipped in the shower."

Miss Ginger stared her down. "The truth," she said after a moment.

"He just gets a little worked up about things sometimes—but it's because he loves me so much."

"So he hurts you because he loves you?"

"I'm not hurt. It's nothing. Just a couple of bruises."

"Love doesn't involve physical injury. This is serious!"

"I'm fine! Really. You're just like everyone else—no one understands our relationship."

"Oh yes, I do. Layla, you're not going to want to hear this, but I think you need to separate yourself from anybody who hurts you."

"But I hurt *him*! I was all up in Justin's face. He was just trying to show me how much that pained him. I shouldn't have been dancing with Justin like that—I deserved it."

"Do you hear yourself, how wrong that sounds? *Nobody* deserves to be abused, Layla. Ever. You need help." Miss Ginger paused, then added, "Maybe more than I can offer."

"I'm not abused. That's women who get beat up. Donny would never hit me."

"He choked you."

"No, he didn't! He stopped!"

"Really? Seriously, Layla?"

Layla sank down on the floor. "It's just, I'm crazy about him . . . and I'm scared I'm losing him. He wants me to quit dance."

"I see. So you'd stop doing the one thing you really love for a guy you *think* you love."

"You make me sound stupid."

"I'm just listening and trying to make sense of what you're saying."

"He's been hanging around with another girl at school—just to make me jealous."

"Is it working?"

"Oh, yeah. The thought of him with her makes me want to puke."

"Did you ever think that maybe Donovan is also a little jealous of you?"

Layla considered this. "Well, I know he hates Justin. He watches through the window, and he hates it when I dance with him."

"I know. I've seen him. Most folks come inside to watch. He seems to like lurking in the shadows."

"Donny is a very private person, and he's a little shy."

"That's probably not a word I'd use to describe him, but go on."

"He told me he wanted me to quit dance—to prove I love him."

Miss Ginger nodded slowly, then turned on "Heaven & Earth" by Kelly Rowland and began to move across the floor. Layla sat in front of the now squeaky-clean mirrors and watched. The music spoke: "'*Cause I know my worth/ And oh, oh, I will no longer settle for whatever . . .*"

Her teacher seemed to melt into the music. The music flowed through her and from her as she leaped across the floor. She was a candle flickering in the wind. Then she was the wind, and as the music slowed, the candle sputtered and disappeared. She fell to the floor in a graceful heap.

"Wow," Layla exclaimed.

Miss Ginger sat up and looked directly at Layla. "I love dance. It is part of my spirit, my essence. It defines who I am. I think the same is true for you. I've seen your face when you take the stage. You light up. You glow. Now *that's* love."

Miss Ginger chose another selection from her iPod, the "Dance of the Swans" from Tchaikovsky's *Swan Lake*, and turned the music up loud. "Dance it out, Layla. Dance."

Layla breathed in the music—it felt to her like some sort of mystical enchantment as she moved. The music pulsed soft and lovely, so she danced as much with her hands as with her feet. Every gesture was lyrical. Every step, delicate. She felt like she was made of feathers. She was a swan at that moment, searching for beauty.

When the music finally stopped, Layla's neck throbbed at the places where Donovan had squeezed. But the rest of her felt alive and tingled with excitement.

"How do you feel?" Miss Ginger asked.

"Fantastic. I could almost see the water the swan floated on."

"And as you danced I was by the side of that lake with you. You have a gift, Layla."

"I don't think I can live without dancing," Layla admitted.

Miss Ginger nodded thoughtfully. "So, what are you going to do?"

"I'm . . . I'm not sure if I'm brave enough to stand up to Donny. Maybe if I apologize to him . . ."

"He's the one who hurt *you*, remember? It is *he* who must apologize!"

"Yeah, but if I smooth things over, maybe we can work this out."

"You need to stand up to him. Demand some changes. Let him know you won't allow him to put his hands on you ever again."

Layla nodded. "I'm gonna try."

"You have to do more than try, or I'm going to make some phone calls—child protective services, the police, my friend the social worker—I've got quite an arsenal. I can't have my girls being abused. I won't!"

"I understand," Layla said. "I do." She put on her Uggs and grabbed her bag. "Thanks for letting me talk to you today, Miss Ginger. You gave me lots to think about."

"Sometimes we all need a day for R and R. You've got

to learn to embrace how wonderful you are. Got that? But if I hear about you skipping school again, I'll kick your butt. And I want you to let me know about how you're handling those other issues, you hear me? I'm not going to wait before I make those phone calls." Miss Ginger gave Layla a big hug.

"Gotcha."

"Now go home and get yourself together. I'll see you at class tonight, right?"

"Right." Layla paused at the front door of the studio. "Miss Ginger?"

"Yes?"

"You know the girl he's seeing at school is named Magnificent? Can you believe that? Her full name is Magnificent Significant Jones."

"Good Lord. Is she all that?"

"She's got the body to match the name."

Miss Ginger laughed. "I bet she can't dance like a feather on a breeze. But you can."

29

JUSTIN, *Tuesday, April 16   12 p.m.*

"'The last thing he ever said to me was,
"Just always be waiting for me, and then some night you will hear me crowing."'"
—from *Peter Pan*

The school lunchroom was hot and crowded, as usual. Justin had to dodge ketchup packets on the floor, book bags in the aisles, and kids tossing French fries as he made his way through the cafeteria.

He noticed Zac and Ben hovering at a table to his left.

"So let me hold them fries," Zac was saying to a skinny, flustered ninth-grader.

"And I'll have those chocolate chip cookies," Ben added, hovering behind Zac as usual.

The younger boy looked around in desperation.

Justin pushed past three kids and shouted, "Back off, Zac!"

Zac spun around, a snarl on his face, but he stepped back when he saw it was Justin. "You suck," he spat out.

"You wanna suck the floor of this nasty cafeteria in front of everybody?" Justin asked, narrowing his eyes.

Zac didn't reply. Without warning, he reached over and snatched the kid's fries. He then bolted out of the lunchroom, with Ben trailing behind like smoke.

The freshman whispered his thanks to Justin, then hunkered over what was left of his lunch. Justin looked around for Mercedes and Steve.

They were sitting in the back near the door, sharing a salad.

Steve looked up. "'Sup?" he said.

Justin slid awkwardly onto the bench that was attached to the cafeteria table. "I hate eating in here. My legs don't fit under these tables. What did they build them for—fifth-graders?"

Steve, even taller and broader than Justin, nodded in agreement. "I feel ya."

"You heard anything new about Diamond?" Justin asked Mercedes.

"No. My mom talks to her mom a couple of times a day, but I don't think there's anything to report."

"No news is good news, right?" Justin took a bite of his burger.

"No news means we still have no idea where she is. I don't think that's good. It's still on all the news stations. But all they keep showing is that video of her mom and dad, crying, begging for her safe return."

Steve looked angry. "Nobody who steals a kid is going to pay attention to crying parents. If he had a heart, he wouldn't have taken her in the first place."

"You're right. Her mom looks really bad," Mercedes said sadly.

Justin thought Mercedes was looking pretty stressed as well—sunken shadows under her eyes, ashen skin, her hair barely combed and falling wildly out of one thin pink scrunchie. She got up and tossed the rest of the salad in the trash.

When she sat back down she whispered to Justin, "Don't turn around, but here comes Donovan and his Transformers doll."

"What do I care?" Justin said, taking another bite of his sandwich.

"Because he's not with Layla, that's why."

"She's not here today. I checked first thing this morning."

"Of course you did."

"Something wrong with that?"

Mercedes shook her head. "The only thing that's wrong is you won't tell Layla how you feel about her."

"She's with Donny. She seems to be locked into that dude."

"Not today. He seems more than a little bit unlocked today. OMG! He's kissing Mag's neck!"

Justin gave her a look. "He's doing it on purpose. He knows you're going to text her and tell."

"I already did. Sent her a couple of messages this morning to let her know what he was doing. But I gotta text this—maybe it will help her shake that dude."

Steve and Justin simply shook their heads.

"You realize you're doing exactly what Donny wants you to do. He's trying to make Layla jealous," Justin told her. "Plus, isn't it a little mean to send her this stuff?"

"Layla thinks Donovan loves her," Mercedes tried to explain. "The girl's got issues. Instead of getting jealous of Donny and his 'Magnificent Significant Mama,' she needs to dump him!"

Steve rubbed her arm gently. "Mercedes, I get what you're doing, but just leave it alone and let her figure it out herself," he advised.

"It might help if *someone* ever made a move," Mercedes said, glaring at Justin.

Justin shrugged. "I tried. I called her."

"Seriously? What happened?"

"She talked to me like I was the computer repairman. Polite, but distant."

"Well, it's a start at least," Mercedes said. "You gotta call her again."

Justin held up both his hands. "I don't know. She blew me off and hung up so she could call Donovan and tell him her good news."

"What news?"

"She was really excited. It seems her dad is being

released—he's coming home real soon—maybe this week."

"Hey, that's awesome! I gotta call her and get all the details."

Justin thrummed his fingers on the lunchroom table, stealing looks at Donovan and Magnificent. "Layla deserves so much better than that guy."

"Like you, maybe?" Mercedes teased.

"Like me, for sure."

"Then *tell* her."

"I will."

"When?"

"Soon."

"Hold still." The flash on her cell cam blazed on and off. "I'm texting her your picture also."

"What are you going to say with the pic?"

She made a mischievous face. "How about 'Justin wants to dance with you'?"

Steve groaned. He picked up his book bag and Mercedes' as well.

Justin made a face. "You're a mess. I feel like I'm back in elementary school, with little girls giggling and passing notes about me."

When the bell rang, the cafeteria emptied quickly. As Donovan strolled toward the doors with Magnificent, he turned and waved at their table, making sure the three of them saw the tat on his arm—the one that said "Layla" in elaborate blue script.

30

LAYLA, *Tuesday, April 16   3 p.m.*

"Oh, the lonely!"

—from *Peter Pan*

Layla twirled her green umbrella and hummed one of the melodies from *Swan Lake* as she walked from the bus stop to her house. But the humming and walking stopped abruptly. Donovan was sitting on the steps in front of her house. He was soaking wet.

"Where you been all day?" he asked.

"Out. Thinking. I stopped and did a little shopping."

"You skipped school."

"It's none of your business."

"You *are* my business."

"Maybe not anymore."

"Aw, don't say that." Rain dripped down his forehead. His shirt stuck to his chest.

"How long have you been sitting out here?"

"A couple of hours."

"Why didn't you just wait in your car?"

"'Cause I wanted to show you how sorry I was about last night." His eyes were red-rimmed, pleading.

"By getting soaked?"

"Yeah." He sneezed. "I'm so, so sorry, Layla. I promise it will never happen again."

"So sorry you had to spend all day drooling all over Magnificent?"

"You know she don't mean nothin' to me. It's just, I was so angry at you."

"Angry at *me*? You trippin'! *I'm* the one who should be upset. And I am."

"I know. I know. But you gotta forgive me."

"You tried to choke me." She yanked down the turtleneck. "You gave me *bruises*! *And* you tried to make me look like a fool while you slobbered all over Mag."

"I told you, I don't care nothin' about Magnificent."

"Then why?"

"I figured if you can dance with Justin, I should be able to dance with Magnificent."

"She can't dance."

"You know what I mean."

"No, I do not."

"I wanted to hurt your feelings. Make you jealous." He sneezed again.

"Do I *look* jealous?" She stood with arms crossed, fierce in her anger.

"Not really. Anyway, she laughs like a hyena, and her underarms smell like onions!"

Layla had to stifle a laugh. "Serves you right." She looked at him, at the water dripping from his hair, his eyebrows, and sighed. "Come on inside and warm up."

"Your mom at home?" he asked as she unlocked the front door.

"No, she's got another double shift."

"Good, that gives us more time alone."

"We need to talk, and that is *all*," Layla said tersely.

"Okay," he said. "You're right."

Surprised at how agreeable he was being, she asked, "You hungry?"

"For you." He flopped down on the sofa.

Her eyes shot daggers. "Don't even go there."

"I'm cool. I'm straight. It's all about you right now." He pulled a hoodie from his gym bag and ripped off his wet T-shirt.

Layla inhaled sharply—he was *so* gorgeous—it turned her to pudding. When his sweatshirt was on, she asked him if he wanted some spaghetti.

"Yeah, nuke me a bowl. You got cheese to melt on that?"

"Extra cheese, coming right up." Layla relaxed a bit and headed for the kitchen.

"This sure beats Mickey D's," he hollered to her.

She came back out with two cold colas and handed

him one. "My health teacher says fast food rots your bones and your brain."

"Probably true."

"Maybe that's why they make it taste so good."

They sat on the sofa in silence for a moment, sipping the sodas. The microwave beeped. Layla jumped up, but Donny placed his hand gently on her arm. "Uh, hey, Layla."

"Yeah."

"I really am sorry about last night."

"You already apologized."

"I just want to make sure we're straight and you're not mad at me. How can I show you how sorry I am?" He reached out.

She backed away a couple of inches. "You've got to make some promises to me, Donny."

"Like what?"

"No more putting your hands on me. Ever. I mean it."

"I promise. Promise. Promise."

"And I'm a dancer. I dance. It is what I do. It is what I am."

"I know. I get it."

"And I am *not* going to quit. You have to live with that." She stood up and crossed her arms.

He looked up at her and grinned slyly. "Do I have to come to recitals?

She narrowed her eyes. "You have to sit in the front row and bring me flowers—every show."

"Seriously?" The alarm on his face made her crack up.

"Kidding. But I'd like to have you there, even if you sit in the back."

He exhaled loudly. "Whew!" He patted the sofa for her to sit down again.

"You're such a mess." But even as she said that, she felt so much better—strong, finally in control.

Donny played with the rip in her jeans. "Do I have to watch you dance with Justin?"

Layla did not remove his hand. But she said firmly, "He is just a guy in dance class. He is nobody to me—you're all I care about. Don't you know that by now?"

"So I don't have to stomp him?"

"You better not!"

"Why? 'Cause you like him?"

"No, because you'd look awful in jail clothes!"

"Like your dad?"

"Don't go there," she hissed.

"Sorry. My bad. I keep messin' up, and all I want to do is be good to you." He eased closer to her. He pulled down the edge of the turtleneck and gently kissed the bruises on her neck.

"I'm so sorry," he murmured. "I swear, I will never hurt you again."

"Promise?"

"I swear on my life." He kissed her once more.

"The spaghetti is getting cold," she whispered.

"I don't care. Seems like I remember you owing me. . . ."

She drew back. "No, Donny. No." But Donny pulled her closer and kissed her ear.

"C'mon, Layla. Prove you're not mad at me anymore. Prove you love me."

Layla went icy cold. She thought about all she and

Miss Ginger had talked about. It was time she stood her ground. She pushed him away. "How about if you show *me* how much you love me instead?"

"That's what I'm trying to do!" He looked more confused than angry.

"I just want some hugs and cuddles tonight. Nothing more. I mean it."

"Seriously?"

"I'm just trying to show you how to make *me* happy for a change."

"By just hugging? You been reading *Teen Vogue* again?"

"Didn't you just ask me how you could show me how sorry you were for almost choking the life outta me?"

"It wasn't that bad."

"Yeah, it was. You scared me. And it hurt."

He ran his fingers through her hair. "You are so right, Layla. I was wrong. Totally wrong. Can you forgive me—for everything?"

Layla looked at him as if he were another person. "You're blowing my mind."

"I'm tryin' here. Can we start over?"

Layla gave him a long look, took in his pleading eyes, and finally said, "We can try, if you'll look at things from my point of view."

"Fair enough. I'm willin'."

Layla felt a happiness she hadn't felt for days, and scooted closer to him. "This really means a lot to me," she told him.

"Wait a sec—you look so *good* sitting there on the

sofa." He took out his cell phone. "Let me take your picture. Smile!"

She smiled. He snapped.

"One more," he said. "Man, you are so fine!" He snapped two more as she grinned happily. He leaned in to kiss her. Slowly. Gently. "I love you, Layla."

Layla's breath caught. He loved her! "That's the first time you've ever said that," she murmured.

"Let me make up for lost time. I love you." He kissed her right ear. "I love you." He kissed her left ear. "I love you." He kissed her nose. "I love you." He kissed her lips again and again.

She kissed him back, feeling like she was pure air, floating.

"I couldn't bear to lose you," he said. "You're the only good thing in my life." He kissed her lips again, then each eyelid. She pressed closer to him.

He tugged up the bottom of her turtleneck, and when she raised her arms, he deftly slipped it over her head.

"This is what I see when you're onstage. Costume tops not much bigger than a bra. I can't help it if I want all this beauty to myself." Once more, he kissed the bruises on her neck. "Beautiful, beautiful, beautiful Layla," he kept repeating between each kiss.

"You think I'm beautiful?"

"Drop-dead gorgeous." And as he said it, that's how she felt—gorgeous. And as he took more pictures, she felt more beautiful still.

"I love you, Donny." He'd never been so gentle, so

genuine. She pressed against him, and he slid his hands up her sides.

"Take off your bra," he whispered.

She didn't try to stop him as he reached behind her and quickly unhooked it.

"So lovely," he whispered. "My lovely Layla."

He touched her almost reverently. He took three more photos. Four. Maybe five. She lay languidly on the sofa pillows, smiling and posing for each shot.

Finally, he closed the phone and slipped it in his back pocket. Then he pulled her shirt from the floor and carefully slipped it over her head. He kissed her once more, then said, "See? I can control myself. I'm trying to show you I'm sorry and how much I love you. Now let's finish off that spaghetti. I don't want you to be late for class tonight."

Layla sprinkled lots of extra cheese in his bowl.

31

MERCEDES, *Wednesday, April 17   9 a.m.*

"'Pan, who and what art thou?' he cried huskily.

"'I'm youth, I'm joy,' Peter answered at a venture,

"'I'm a little bird that has broken out of the egg.'"

—from *Peter Pan*

"How's Diamond's family doing?" Layla asked Mercedes the next day as they huddled in the front hall, waiting for the bell to ring for first period. Layla, dressed mostly in yellow, from the rings on her fingers to her funky bejeweled flip-flops, seemed to be bubbling. Mercedes wondered what was up with that.

"Falling apart. Shasta's been wetting her bed. My mom says Mrs. Landers has stopped eating. Mr. Landers has this faraway look on his face—like he's looking right through you—it's a little creepy. He leaves at the crack of dawn every morning to look for Diamond."

"Where does he go?"

"He keeps going back to the mall, I guess hoping the man who took Diamond will come back. Shasta told me the mall had received complaints about a strange, unshaven man who stares at folks like they're guilty of something," Mercedes told her.

"I can't believe it's been four whole days and we have no clues, no word—nothing," Steve said.

"On TV they said the longer someone is missing, the less likely it is to find them . . . That freaks me out," Layla said.

"Yeah, well, I gotta believe she's alive and will come back to us somehow. I just gotta." Mercedes shifted her backpack.

"Give it here," Steve said, putting it over his shoulder. "Man, this thing weighs a ton! And hey, nice 'fit today, Layla. What did you do—clean out the yellow section in your closet? I gotta get out my shades to combat the shine you're bouncing."

"I feel bad that I'm so happy, when Diamond is still missing," Layla said, smoothing the edge of the black turtleneck under her shimmery top. A black sparkled butterfly seemed to flutter in the center of her shirt as she moved.

"That butterfly looks like it's about to land in a plate of butter," Mercedes teased her. "What's up with you?"

"Lots of good stuff. Me and Donny are *so* straight, *so* good, *so* tight." Her eyes glistened, and she did a tiny elevé, almost standing on her toes.

Mercedes waited patiently. "Go on."

"And my father is coming home! Yellow is his favorite color."

"That explains it. Hey, that's great! It's been a long time." Mercedes didn't mention that she'd already heard the news.

"Way too long. I'm kinda nervous."

"It'll be easier than you think—don't worry. So, where *is* Donny this morning? And what did he do to make you flitter like that bug on your shirt?"

Layla shook her head. "Oh, Donny never comes to first bell. But he'll be here soon. He just texted me."

"You still didn't tell me how he made you so happy."

"He told me he loved me. He loves me!" She twirled happily, nearly bumping into Justin, who had just walked up.

"Why do they make us wait out here like a herd of animals?" Justin complained. "If they just let us go to our lockers when we get to school, they wouldn't have to worry about crowd control."

"That's your key word—control," Steve reasoned. "They think they gotta keep us corralled or something. But isn't it way past time for the bell? What's going on?"

Mercedes checked her watch. "You're right. It's almost nine o'clock!"

Zizi appeared from nowhere and squeezed between Layla and Justin. "Oh my God! Guess what I just heard?" she announced breathlessly.

"If there's drama, you know about it," Mercedes said.

"The reason they're keeping us out here is because there is an escaped criminal with a *bomb* in the school!"

"Oh, be for real," Layla said.

"No, seriously. I saw cop cars out front, and bomb-sniffing dogs!"

"Maybe they were drug-sniffing dogs," Steve offered. "I can bet you big money that we have more drugs than bombs in this school."

"Don't they do random drug sweeps every once in a while?" Layla asked.

"Yeah, and they never find anything. The druggies know how to hide their stuff," Mercedes said in disgust.

Just then the school PA system trilled. Everyone quieted to listen to the principal give the announcement.

"Good morning, students. Please pardon our delay in starting school today. Our health team has been given a mandate to check the building for ants and termites. Yes, I know. This could have been done after school hours, but we have to follow orders from the central office. This shouldn't take long, so relax and enjoy the time. We will probably cancel first bell completely and start our day with bell two. For now, I'm going to play some music to keep you mellow while you wait. Have a great day."

"Seriously?" Zizi asked, her hands on her hips. "Bugs? Bombs would have been way more interesting! Besides, bugs make me itch. In fact, I'm itching right now!" She began to scratch at her arms and legs.

"Mrs. Gennari is cool for a principal," Mercedes said, shaking her head at Zizi. "I like that she's straight with us."

The music began to play—loud and energizing. The PA speakers were tinny at best, but Mercedes was impressed that Mrs. Gennari had chosen a song they all actually listened to.

"Good thing Mrs. G. has a teenage daughter," Layla said, beginning to shimmy. "Otherwise we'd be probably listening to oldies from the sixties!"

"You look nice today," Justin said to Layla. "That yellow makes you, I don't know, uh, kinda glow."

"Like a light bulb," Mercedes joked.

"What I mean to say, Layla," Justin continued, fixing Mercedes a quit-it glance, "is that color brings out the best in you. You look really nice."

"Thanks, Justin," Layla replied. "I guess I'm just happy today." She spun into a little whirl in the midst of the crowd of kids.

"I'm going to the studio right after school to get in some practice," Justin told Layla. Mercedes hid a smile as she watched him try to break past Layla's defenses. "You want to meet me there and go over the duo Miss Ginger suggested we try? I think it will be a great competition piece."

Mercedes caught Justin's eye and nodded with approval.

But Layla shut the idea down. "I might not get to class tonight, Justin. I told you, my dad is coming home. I'm waiting for a phone call from my mother, who *finally* told me about his release. If she gets the final approval from the corrections bureau this morning, she's taking off work today to go and get him. I want to be there when he walks in the door."

"I feel ya," Justin replied with a shrug. "It's cool."

A new song came over the loudspeaker, and several of the students began to dance. "This feels like one of those crazy scenes from that movie *Fame*," Zizi said. "I didn't think it could happen in real life. This is awesome." She grabbed a very surprised freshman, who eventually grinned and danced with her, matching her steps. The gauzy pale purple blouse she was wearing floated around her effortlessly. Mercedes joined them, moving to the beats that emanated from the speakers.

Eventually, Steve and the rest of the kids in the hall began to back away to make room as the dance academy students gravitated to the center and basically took over. Jillian appeared from nowhere; her elegant moves immediately drew attention. Kids clapped as each dancer did her thing. Zizi. Mercedes. Layla. Jillian.

When Chris Brown's "Kiss Kiss" blared from the speakers, the kids in the crowd cheered and backed away farther as Justin took over the center. He popped. He locked. He flipped. He spun. His classmates went wild, stomping and hooting. Mercedes watched Layla tap her feet as she watched Justin dance.

Another song began. "Just the Way You Are" by Boyce Avenue. It was slower, more sensuous. Breathing hard, Justin extended his hand to Layla. She smiled and reached out her hand to him. They moved together, almost as if they were one person. They twisted and stepped together. He twirled her around, then gently lifted her while the music surged around them. The words to the song were so perfect for Layla—for the two of them, Mercedes thought. *"It's so sad to think she don't see what I see . . ."*

Layla landed delicately and spun within the circle of Justin's arms. For a moment, there was only Justin, Layla, and the music that swirled around them. The kids in the crowd were silent, mesmerized by the beauty of the dance. And then—

"What the hell?!" Donovan was pushing his way through the clog of students. He grabbed Layla roughly and jerked her away from Justin.

"Donny? What's wrong?" Layla asked, trying to twist her wrist out of his grasp.

"You askin' me what's wrong? I show up and find my girl showin' her stuff and rubbin' up against this dude. In front of everybody! How dare you?"

"Donny, you're embarrassing me." Her face flushed, and she said beseechingly, "Let's talk about this later."

"No. We deal with this now!"

Mercedes tried to intervene. "All of us were dancing, Donny. It was just something to do until the bell rang."

"This ain't got nothin' to do with you, Mercedes. Now back off," Donny snapped. He continued to squeeze Layla's wrist while she clawed at his hand with her other hand.

Mercedes glanced toward Steve. *Do something,* she mouthed.

The music continued to play, but somehow the foyer

felt deathly quiet. The students looked uneasy, eyeing each other, no one making a move.

No one, except Justin. Looking like he could take no more, he stormed over to Donovan, grabbed his hand, and peeled his fingers from Layla's wrist.

Mercedes grasped Layla's arm and drew her away. Layla peered at her reddened wrist, Donovan's fingers clearly outlined on her skin.

"Keep your hands off her!" Justin shouted, his nostrils flaring.

"She belongs to me, and you, dance boy, won't tell me what to do!" Donovan lurched forward and grabbed Layla's wrist again to prove the point.

Layla jerked her arm away.

Justin glared at him. "She is nobody's property. Slavery was abolished a long time ago."

"Layla is my woman. And I can prove it."

Layla's eyes went wide. "No. No. No," she whispered.

"Correction," Justin said. "Layla is a lady. She should be treated like one."

Donovan smirked. "You might be wrong about Miss High and Mighty here. She might not be the angel you think she is."

"Donovan . . . No, baby. . . . Please, no," Layla begged.

Mercedes couldn't understand why Layla looked so horrified.

"Layla deserves better than scum like you, Donovan," Justin spat out.

"Don't be callin' me names now. Don't make me have to tighten you up."

"I ain't scared of you," Justin shot back.

"This ain't got nothin' to do with you, Justin. I know how to handle my women, and you can't stop me."

"I can. And I will."

"Just try it, you little dance fag."

Mercedes held her breath.

Justin's eyes narrowed. He tightened his fist, pulled back his arm, and let Donovan have it, right below his left eye.

The crowd gasped.

Donovan, unbelievably, staggered, then fell to his knees. He looked around in confusion. And anger.

A few kids clapped at Justin's success, but most backed off as they saw the fury emanating from Donovan.

Justin snatched up his book bag and melted into the crowd.

32

DIAMOND, *Wednesday, April 17   9 a.m.*

"By and by there was to be heard a sound at once the most musical and the most melancholy in the world: the mermaids calling to the moon."
—from *Peter Pan*

I want to die, was Diamond's first thought as she woke up on the fourth morning. Aching from the abuse of the night before, she could barely move. Her arms were now untied, but as she glanced at the rope burns, deep and raw, she knew they probably needed medical attention. She lay there, remembering horrible images, trying to forget. She was glad he'd drugged her, because she didn't want to know what the men had done to her that made her struggle that hard.

Oh God, please take me from this place, she prayed.

When Thane had brought her dinner the night before, he had told her, "The drugs are in the bottle of water. Less than usual. I want you more conscious. Drink it if you want. But"—and here he leered at her—"you might want to be more awake tonight. You're a natural, Diamond. I can tell you enjoy it."

Diamond had screamed with rage. "I hate this! I hate this! I hate you! I want OUT of here!"

"Not yet. You're still too valuable—you're making me a boatload of money."

"How?" She wanted to know. She didn't want to know. "No, don't tell me."

He did anyway. "Men pay me to come here and be with you on camera. Men and women both pay me to watch you online. You're so much more . . . ah . . . pliable than any of the other girls I've worked with. You're quite a draw—my bestseller, in fact—you should be very proud of yourself."

"*Other* girls?" Diamond's head was spinning.

"Oh, yes. You are the first from around here, but I've filmed dozens of dumb kids like you. In my line of work I have to keep moving, as you might imagine."

"Where are these other girls now?" Diamond hardly dared to think of the possibilities.

"I don't know, and I don't care."

"None of them turned you in?"

"Not a one."

"Why not?"

Thane raised his eyebrows arrogantly. "What difference does it make?"

Diamond slumped back, fighting the hollowness of despair that was threatening to overwhelm her. She tried to reason with him. "Look, it doesn't have to be now, it doesn't have to be today, but tell me you'll let me go. I'll be just like those other girls. I won't say a word. I promise."

He ignored her, swiping on his phone as it rang. "Yes," he said, his voice slimy. "She *is* delicious. She'll be ready at seven." He put the phone back into his pocket.

Diamond closed her eyes, trying to think. She needed a way to overpower him, beat him up, make him stop. Nothing. Nothing. Nothing.

"I like you, Diamond," he continued. "I'm thinking I might take you with me. I'm thinking of heading to Colorado next. I bet you'll really like the mountains."

Diamond's eyes grew wide with horror. "No. Don't take me away. You've gotta let me go home, Thane. Please. I can't do this anymore."

"Sure you can. You're a keeper, Diamond. And you're going to do everything I say."

"No!" She threw her flip-flop across the room at him, but he ducked easily.

"Oh, you will." He cocked his head as if pondering something. "I drove by your house the other day. How old is your sister—about nine?"

"NO!" Diamond screamed. "You keep your filthy hands off her!"

"I've got customers who prefer them young."

"No! Don't you *dare* touch her!"

"Do you know how easy it is to pick up a kid? I've got this wonderful dog that is both handsome and charming. Pulling a kid into a van with Bella is, well, child's play." He curled his lips into a gruesome smile.

"You couldn't. You wouldn't," Diamond choked out, trying not to break down.

"Oh, I can and I will. Shasta will get her chance to star in movies, just like you. Hah! A sister act—I love it!"

Diamond screamed and screamed and screamed.

Thane waited. "Or . . . you cooperate. Colorado's gorgeous this time of year."

"Please don't touch my baby sister," Diamond moaned. "I'll do anything you want."

"Drugs are in the water. Drink it or not. Your choice. You can be a junkie, or you can be clearheaded and enjoy the experience." He shut and locked the door.

Diamond stared at the bottle for a long, long time.

33

LAYLA, *Wednesday, April 17   10 a.m.*

"For the moment she had forgotten his ignorance about kisses."
—from *Peter Pan*

Layla sat on the floor in the girls' bathroom, head in her hands, sobbing. Mercedes tried to comfort her, but Layla only pushed her away.

"You upset because Justin hit Donovan?" Mercedes asked.

Layla shook her head.

"You angry because Donny acted like a caveman?"

Layla shook her head again.

"Then what's wrong, girl? You know I got your back."

Layla looked up, her eyes rimmed with running mascara. Mercedes handed her a paper towel from the dispenser.

Layla blew her nose. "It started out as such a great day."

"It still is, Layla. Look at it this way—you've got *two* dudes fighting over you."

"I never asked for Justin to fight for me. Now things are totally messed up."

"I don't get it. Donovan can't be all up in your face like that—Justin was like a superhero or something, jumping in right when you needed it."

"Why couldn't he just leave us alone?" She kicked at the wastebasket.

"Layla, you're telling me you'd rather get smacked around in public by Donovan than get defended by a gentleman like Justin?"

"Donny didn't smack me."

"He squeezed the hell out of your wrist. Look at the marks!"

Layla glanced down. "That's nothin'. He didn't hurt me. He was just jealous because I was dancing with Justin."

"And that gives him the right to yell at you in public and treat you like his personal property? Justin was right. Slavery's over, girl."

"I was so happy this morning," Layla wailed.

"It's still early. You've got the whole day to get it back. Maybe now Donny will think twice about putting his hands on you."

Layla shouted, "No!" She pounded the bathroom stall again and again. "You don't get it. He *will not* get over this. He'll try to get even."

"You think he'll try to really hurt you?"

Layla gave her a hollow gaze. Mercedes *so* didn't get it. "In ways you can't even imagine."

"You're scaring me, girl. What do you mean?"

Layla's lips quivered. "I can't tell you."

Mercedes paused. "I'm here for you—you know that, right?"

"I gotcha."

"Well, for now, blow your nose again, and let's get to class. Mr. Baxson is gonna have a hernia."

Layla stood up and brushed the dust off her skirt. Picking up her book bag, she followed Mercedes down the hall.

She dreaded what the rest of the day would bring. Because she knew Donovan. No way was he going to let this slide. No way.

34

LAYLA, *Wednesday, April 17 5 p.m.*

"In the end she grew up of her own free will a day quicker than other girls."
—from *Peter Pan*

Layla sat in a corner of the studio with her head down, her knees pulled up to her chest, and her arms wrapped around her legs. Her biology book sat unopened beside her. She didn't look up, but anybody within a ten-mile radius could hear Zizi's cheerful chatter.

Zizi had swooped over to Justin as soon as he walked in. "Hey, hero man. If you want, I'll run up to the costume closet and see if I can find a cape for you. You are awesome, man. Awesome. I bow down to you." And then she did.

"Will you get up, you nut? Chill." Justin tossed his backpack into a corner.

"But it's all everybody is talking about!" she told him excitedly. "Donovan went home right after you clocked his socks—too embarrassed to show his face, I guess."

"Stop, Zizi, please." Justin held up a hand.

"Check your Facebook page, Justin. Plus, I happen to know five girls personally who want to hook up with you. I bet you get offers to star in a movie! I can see it now—you riding in on a white horse. No, in a white Benz."

"Thanks, Zizi, but it's not like all that. I got sent home—I'll probably get suspended tomorrow. My dad is gonna be real disappointed."

Layla raised her eyebrows, but continued to sit quietly, ignoring them both.

"What! No way! That's so not fair. I would think they'd give you a reward for putting Donovan Beaudry in his place!"

"Yeah. You'd think."

"Well, I still think you should check your Facebook page." She glanced over at the corner. "Unless you'd rather check on Layla."

"Let me focus on my dancing right now, okay, Zizi?" Justin pleaded.

Layla kept her head down, trying to look like she hadn't just been listening to them. Justin walked over. "Can I sit down?" he asked.

"You don't need my permission," she said, frowning.

She wasn't sure if Justin was good news or just plain trouble.

"I want to apologize for embarrassing you," he began.

"Not necessary."

"I could have handled that better," he said.

"You think?"

"I'm gonna get suspended."

Layla shifted her legs. "I heard. So is Donovan, even though he never touched you."

Justin nodded slowly. "Maybe he's getting suspended for touching *you*."

"Maybe."

Justin shifted his position on the floor. "Layla, look at me."

She raised her head.

"I'm not sorry for smacking Donovan down. I'd do it again. You are like this . . . this . . . exotic flower, and he treats you like the dirt in the garden. It drives me crazy."

"Wow. That was pretty poetic." She looked at Justin thoughtfully—maybe Mercedes was right. Maybe he ran deeper than she'd been willing to admit.

He admitted sheepishly, "I got more!"

She let herself smile. "Spare me, please."

"Seriously, Layla, I love dancing with you. When we dance together, it's, like, I don't know, like, *dazzling*. I don't want anything to spoil that."

Hah. She had plenty to spoil everything. But instead she just said, "Well, you *are* the best male dancer in our class."

He cracked up. "I'm the *only* male dancer in our class."

She picked up her biology book and stuffed it in her bag. "Look, I really like dancing with you, too, Justin. I feel like I dance better when I dance with you." She paused. "But I've got some serious issues to deal with. I'm not the perfect little daisy you imagine." She gave him a challenging stare. "Things are gonna happen that will change your opinion of me. I don't want you to get caught up in my mess."

"I'm not following," Justin said, frowning.

"You will. Soon." Layla hopped up, and joined Mercedes on the other side of the studio, and began to stretch.

"Hey, girl, I thought you weren't coming to class because your dad was coming home," Mercedes said.

"Mom called and said it will probably be tomorrow," Layla said with a sigh. "I got all dressed up for nothing. But I'd rather be here than at home, alone."

"Gotcha."

When Miss Ginger started the class, Layla kept her distance from Justin. She did the routines as requested, but nothing more.

When they stopped for a water break, Mercedes dug into her bag for her phone. "Gotta send a text to Steve," she told Layla with a grin.

"You two are a trip." Layla sipped her water listlessly and glanced out the window at the darkening skies. She turned her head when she heard Mercedes stifle a scream.

"Oh my God!" Mercedes blurted out. "Oh, no!"

"What's up?" Layla asked. Could there be news about Diamond? But no. Somehow she knew. She just knew.

"I can't!"

"Can't what?

"I can't show you!"

"You're talkin' crazy. Can't show me what? Something from Steve?" Layla hoped against hope.

"Sit down, Layla. This is bad. Really bad."

"Is it a text?" Layla whispered.

"Yeah."

"A picture?"

"Yeah."

"Of me?" He couldn't have, could he? . . . He wouldn't have. . . .

Mercedes nodded miserably. "Three of them. Check your phone, Layla. Now!"

Layla hesitated, then reached into her bag and opened her phone. She screamed as she read the message from Donovan.

this is going out 2 evrybdy u no. u slut. u whore.

Attached to the message were three color photos of Layla—smiling, posing, and bare-breasted.

35

MERCEDES, *Wednesday, April 17   7 p.m.*

"He could only stare, horrified."
—from *Peter Pan*

Mercedes watched helplessly as Layla flung her cell phone across the floor and collapsed in ragged, gulping sobs. She tried to put her arms around Layla's heaving shoulders, but Layla shook her off. The rest of the students in the class hovered at a distance, their faces full of questions.

Miss Ginger hurried over, pulled Layla to her feet, and marched her into her office. "Jillian, continue the class," she ordered, and firmly shut the office door.

Layla's had one rough day, Mercedes thought. First the fight, then finding out her dad wasn't coming home tonight, then this horrible, horrible thing. She'd be bawling too.

Justin, his face full of concern, asked her, "What's wrong with Layla?"

"You didn't see them yet?"

"See what?"

"Just check your text messages. Now."

Justin hurried to dig out his phone. He popped it open. "I got three texts from Donny. What's up with that?"

"Just open them," Mercedes said flatly.

"Oh God, no!" Justin cried out, looking at the photos in disbelief. "Oh, no!"

Mercedes knew what he was seeing—the message with the first picture said, **"layla the slut."** The second said, **"layla the ho."** The third one said, **"layla 4 sale."**

"How *could* he?" Justin choked out.

Mercedes, staggered by the horrible possibility of dozens and dozens of other kids getting Donovan's texts, asked shakily, "What can we do?" She slipped to the floor, staring at her cell phone.

"Delete them," Justin said, his voice icy with anger.

Mercedes, her fingers trembling, hit her delete button. She felt utterly sick. "He probably sent this to everybody at school. Then everyone will forward it to everyone else on their phone lists. It's probably already gone viral."

Justin's chest heaved like he was working hard to

control himself. "What a heartless bastard!" Then he stopped short. "Oh my God!"

"What?" Mercedes asked.

"Those pictures—they'll be out there forever. *Forever*." Justin looked angry enough to break something.

Mercedes closed her eyes, then glanced over at Layla in Miss Ginger's office. *Oh, Layla, girlfriend, this sucks so bad.* She knew Layla probably just wanted to die. "How's she gonna get over this?" she asked Justin.

Jillian, who had cued up a song, was trying vainly to get the class back into order, but nobody seemed to want to dance or pay her much attention.

Ignoring Jillian, Justin continued to fume. "I just want to kill him!"

"You'd have to move to Siberia or something if you did," Mercedes said, trying to calm him down.

Justin would not be sidetracked. "I can't get in that dude's headspace. He says he loves her, and he does *this*? You don't throw this kind of dirt if you really care about someone!"

Hoping against hope he wouldn't say yes, she asked Justin, "Does this, um, change your opinion of Layla?"

Justin looked surprised. "Of course not." He scratched his head. "That dude, he has this crazy control over her. I don't get how he got her to pose like that—but she sure never thought he'd do *this*."

"So, what can we do to help?"

"I'm gonna . . . I'm gonna . . . let her know I'm there for her—that everybody makes mistakes. I can't begin to imagine how embarrassed she must be."

Mercedes looked thoughtful. "She might feel too stressed to deal with dudes for a while. Just sayin'. . . ."

Justin shrugged. "Yeah, probably. And I wouldn't blame her. But I'll be there when she's ready."

"You're awesome, Justin, you know that?" Mercedes poked him in the arm affectionately.

He brushed her comment off. "Hope Layla figures that out too," he said with a shrug.

Just then, Zizi screamed. "OMG! Look at these pictures I just got!"

Justin and Mercedes said at the same time, "Delete them, Zizi! Now!"

She nodded and began pushing keys on her phone.

Jillian finally turned the music off, clearly giving up. "You wanna try?" she asked Mercedes as she sank to the floor.

"Not tonight," Mercedes said, shaking her head.

Just then, Layla, quiet and subdued, came out of Miss Ginger's office. She picked up her phone from the middle of the floor, grabbed her bag, and headed out to the parking lot without speaking to anyone.

36

LAYLA, *Wednesday, April 17   8 p.m.*

"Mrs. Darling put her hand to her heart and cried,
'Oh, why can't you remain like this for ever!'"
—from *Peter Pan*

"I am dirt," Layla said out loud to the damp night sky. "Filthier than dirt." She felt dazed, like she'd just been pushed off a cliff, and she was freefalling to destruction. She didn't know what she could hold on to, who she could trust, or what she could possibly say. She couldn't find the breath to explain anything, couldn't grab any idea that would even begin to make things right. She felt weightless, helpless, broken.

She groaned as she spotted the headlights from her mother's battered Chevy. Why was she here? Layla wiped her face with the back of her hand and pasted on a fake smile as he mother swung into a parking space.

"Layla, what's wrong, hon?" her mother asked as she hopped out of the car. "Have you been crying?"

"I, uh, stubbed my toe in class," Layla said evasively, sniffling just a little. "Let's go. I am so ready to be out of there."

Mrs. Ridgewood reached out and gave her a quick hug. "Well, I've got something to make you feel better—I've got somebody I want you to meet."

Layla groaned for a second time. She was gonna lose it if her mother introduced her to one more random male friend. "Not tonight, Mom. Please."

The passenger door creaked open then, and a tall, bearded man unfolded from the front seat. He stood in the shadows for a moment, as if hesitant.

Layla instantly began to tremble. "Daddy?" she whispered. "Daddy?"

Raphael Ridgewood strode toward her and engulfed her in his arms. "Oh, my sweet baby girl!"

Layla couldn't help herself—she began to cry. Her dad! Home! And he smelled the same as she remembered—like lemonade and leather. He seemed thinner, and shorter, somehow. But maybe she'd grown. His face was covered with a full, scruffy beard.

Her mom tittered nervously, then said, "I came early,

hoping to get here before Donovan did—I wanted to surprise you."

Layla froze at the mention of his name. "He won't be picking me up anymore," she said tersely. "We broke up." Quickly changing the subject, she said, "Mom said you weren't coming until tomorrow. I've missed you so much, Daddy!"

"Well, let's go home," her father said. "We have lots of catching up to do."

Layla crawled into the backseat, her mind awhirl. Donovan. Her dad home. Still no word from Diamond. All of it seemed impossible.

As her mother pulled the car out of the parking lot, her father reached back and said, "I brought you something." He handed her a small chilled cup—a strawberry smoothie.

Layla lost it again. He remembered! After six years. Her heart gave a little leap; maybe he'd remember the curtains! When she finally got control of herself, she whispered, "Thanks, Daddy. My favorite!" When she took a sip, she was ten again and dancing on her porch for her father.

"Thinking of you and your dancing got me through some tough times. I've been counting the days to when I could get you another strawberry smoothie," her father replied. "So, when is your next recital?"

"In June. That's when we're doing a dance version of *Peter Pan*."

"Awesome. I can't wait. What's your part?" her father asked.

Layla's heart gave a second leap. It felt so good to be

telling her dad her good news. "I'm Wendy, the biggest part—next to Peter Pan, I guess." Then an awful thought struck her. What if Miss Ginger was so disgusted at her that she took the lead away? That tiny spark of happiness flickered away.

"The lead! Aw, Layla, I'm so proud of you," her father exclaimed.

"You didn't tell me you got the lead, Layla," her mother said. "That's really cool."

"Uh, I just found out a couple of days ago, and you've been, uh, busy." Layla slid down in the backseat.

"Hey, would you two like to stop and get some Skyline Chili?" her mom asked. Layla felt another small surge of happiness. She was in the car *with her dad*! And she could swear even her mom seemed a little nervous, maybe even a bit excited.

"Oh boy, have I missed Skyline!" her father said enthusiastically. "Absolutely."

As they headed to the chili shop, her father marveled at new buildings that had been built and old buildings that had disappeared since he'd been gone. When they finally got to the apartment, bags of chili and crackers in hand, Layla warned him that it wasn't like their old house.

"It's fine with me, sweetie, as long as you and your mother are there," her father replied. He'd slung one small brown duffel bag over his back.

"It's going to take some adjusting," her mother said nervously. "For all of us."

"I understand, Lillian." He took the bags of food from

her. "I want to take it slow and ease back into your lives. No pressure, okay?"

"I work double shifts most days," she told him.

"And I've got a job already lined up, believe it or not. An old buddy of mine has promised to teach me brick-laying. I can always find work laying bricks." He looked from Layla to her mother. "I'm going to do my part to get back into the swing of things too."

Layla could see the relief on her mother's face. And as the threesome walked up the stairs to the apartment, Layla couldn't stop grinning. For the moment, she set aside her massive problems with Donovan, her massive worry about Diamond, and unlocked their door, welcoming her father into the modest living room. He beamed as he touched the sofa, the chair, the television, the photo of Layla at age three, sitting on his shoulders. He peeked into the kitchen, and then it was his turn to grin. "The yellow curtains!" he exclaimed. "I really am home."

37

DIAMOND, *Thursday, April 18   10 a.m.*

"Stars are beautiful, but they must not take an active part in anything, they must just look on for ever. It is a punishment put on them for something they did so long ago that no star now knows what it was."
—from *Peter Pan*

Diamond had lost track of the time. What day was it? How long had she been in this horrible place? She was beginning to think she wasn't ever, ever getting away.

She hated that she was getting used to the awful routine. A morning shower. New clothes. Fresh sheets. Breakfast with no utensils—just finger food. Often a gift. An iPad loaded with games—no Internet access, of course. A paperback novel. Fresh fruit.

He was bizarrely kind to her each morning, smiling and joking and even bringing Bella in, letting the dog stay for hours at a time. Diamond buried her face into Bella's soft red fur and cried through the afternoons. Bella pressed close and stayed by her side. It helped.

She also hated, *hated* the fact that a tiny little part of her looked forward to Thane's visits in the morning. It was just that she was just so very lonely. Now was that disgusting or what? And what they did to her at night, every night—she refused to even think about the specifics. She couldn't let herself go there. Just when she thought there couldn't possibly be anything worse added, it was. Thane's phone rang constantly. Sometimes he came in two or three times a night with different men. Only the faces changed.

And because he'd been decreasing the amount of drugs in her water each night, she became increasingly and painfully aware of what they were doing to her. And a new horrifying thought obsessed her. What if she got pregnant? Oh, God!

She clung to hope, however. It was all she had. Even though she could see no chance of escape, no chance of ever being found, she stubbornly refused to give up and completely give in. To do that would be to give Thane the final victory. She was *not* letting him have all of her. It simply wasn't going to happen! So she kept hope and faith tucked deep inside, hidden from him.

She did let herself wonder how her parents were

doing. Had they done one of those tearful abduction statements for the news? She'd never paid much attention to those kind of news stories. She had listened, distracted, while arguing with Shasta over stupid things like who got a bigger brownie for dessert. She'd felt sorry for the families, briefly, but she'd never really thought about how much it had to *hurt*. It was excruciating to think about her strong parents helpless, about her mom probably crying every night, about Shasta, scared.

"How much longer are you keeping me here, Thane?" Diamond asked him, like she'd done every day, when he came in that afternoon after taking Bella for a walk.

"I'm glad you asked. I've found a suitable house in Colorado. I'll be moving out in a couple of days." He looked her up and down and smiled. "I'm getting tired of you anyway. I like my girls fresh and untouched. So do my customers."

What did that mean? One part of her mind sped to: Was he letting her go? The other went much darker—was he going to kill her? And yet another part went toward a nameless other girl who was going to have to go through this nightmare.

"Well, I'm sick and tired of you, too! So *let me go home*!" she demanded, her voice fierce.

"Well, aren't we feeling bold today," he replied mildly, ignoring her outburst. "No, I have a better idea. I have a business partner who has some very . . . ah . . . creative ideas for you. He's seen your films online, and he's anxious to work with you."

"What do you mean?" Her heart began to pound.

221

It was something else she'd refused to let herself think about—the nasty, vile videos of her that were circulating through the underbelly of the Internet. She prayed that none of her friends—or, God forbid, her parents—ever saw any of them. But stuff like that *never* went away, never really got fully deleted. Never.

"He says you're ready for more than just Internet flicks. He wants to make you a full-fledged star in the industry." He glared coldly at her. "You wanted to be a star, remember?"

"The industry?"

"The porn business, stupid. Full-length movies."

Diamond burst out angrily, "But you can't! I'm not like that! I'm not that kind of girl."

Thane laughed outright. "You *used to be* a nice girl. From where I sit, you're a whole different kind of *nice*—and completely broken in."

Diamond felt her face burning.

"He's offered me quite a bit of money for you."

"You're *selling* me?"

"Just passing you along to someone who wants you more. But he's got to make it worth my while."

"I won't do it!"

"Oh, you will. Or your little sister will."

"No! No! No! You can't! You won't!"

"Sure I can. I've told you—it's easy. She gets out of school at 2:35. I walk by with my lovable dog. Bella gets away from me. Shasta helps me catch her. Then I catch Shasta. Piece of cake."

"You've *watched* her?" Diamond asked, incredulous.

"Of course. Your parents, too." He gave a short laugh. "They're a mess."

"Are they . . . are they looking for me?" Diamond couldn't help asking.

"Your father hangs in the mall, hoping to catch a glimpse of me. He sat right next to me in the food court yesterday and didn't even know who I was."

Diamond grabbed her head and screeched, "How do you *know* all this?"

"I watched *you* for weeks before I grabbed you. Correction. Before you walked out of the mall with me quite willingly."

Diamond closed her eyes. She couldn't take this. She *wouldn't* take this!

Thane left the dog when he locked the door. Diamond leaned against her softness all afternoon. She felt so numb she couldn't even cry. The words to a song from the musical *Into the Woods* kept looping through her thoughts.

When the one thing you want/Is the only thing out of your reach.

38

LAYLA, *Thursday, April 18   10 a.m.*

"He has an iron hook instead of a right hand, and he claws with it."
—from *Peter Pan*

It started as soon as she got to school. Layla knew it would. The whispers. The laughter. The propositions. The derision.

She'd had to shut down her Facebook page as it had exploded with nasty comments. As she walked down the hall, it was constant, ceaseless. Some were said just loud enough for her to hear. Others were made directly to her.

From the guys:

"Nice tits."

"Wanna give me some of that?"

"Oo-wee! You made my day!"

"Lettin' it all hang out, I see."

"What else you got?"

"I got a camera. You want to party with me?"

"I got what you want, baby."

"Come on over to my house."

"Bring it on over here to me."

"Hardcore. Umph."

"Lucky man, that Donovan."

"Homie hopper."

"What else you got to show me?"

"The whole football team wants you now."

"I sent your photos to every dude I know. You got more?"

From the girls:

"Stupid ho."

"You don't have much to show off anyway."

"You knew what you was doing."

"If Donny says you a ho, then you a ho."

"That is not the way to keep a man."

"Cheap slut."

"She always fakin' like she's nice."

"I knew she was easy."

"She sure looked like she was enjoying herself."

"Who woulda thought?"

"Lowlife."

"Better quit actin' like you all that!"

"I sent her pics to my cousins in Jersey."

"I posted them on Facebook!"

"Those pics are everywhere."

"This is the best scandal that's happened all year!"

In her classes Layla tried to pay attention, but the rumblings and murmurs never stopped. Her teachers, at least for today, were clueless. They had no idea about the vast network of Internet connections that the students shared. But she knew that sooner or later one of the teachers would find out. And then her parents. It was never going to go away. Never.

When her father found out, he'd be so deeply disappointed. After all those years apart, missing the innocent little girl he'd left behind, he would think that she really was the slut everyone assumed she was.

She skipped Spanish class and found a seat in the back of the auditorium. She sat there alone in that huge, darkened room, wishing she could disappear. And she *knew* how awful that thought was—truly awful, awful, awful—because Diamond actually *had* disappeared. But she didn't know how to deal with this. She had no idea how to make it through, how to make it go away.

The auditorium door opened, letting in a shaft of light. Justin walked in, clearly looking for her. Layla scrunched down, but he spotted her and headed her way. She groaned. He must have followed her and skipped Spanish as well. But she just wanted to be *alone*!

She couldn't do this now. She simply could not face anyone else. But there was no way to get away before he reached her; she was caught.

"What do *you* want, Justin?" she asked, a sharp edge to

her voice. "You want to check and see if my boobs match the pictures?"

"I deleted the photos the moment I received them," Justin replied evenly.

"Why? You don't get turned on when you look at women's breasts?"

"I didn't choose to look at those particular pictures, that's all."

"All the dudes say you're gay. Is that why you deleted the pics?" She knew she was being a butt, but she couldn't stop lashing out at him.

"I'm not gay."

"Everybody else is having a holiday spreading my stuff all over the world."

"I'm not everybody else."

She was amazed at how calm Justin was. So she asked him point-blank, "What do you think of me? Honest answer."

"I think you're beautiful," he said simply. "I thought so from the first time I ever saw you."

"Hah! Never was. Never will be now."

"Nothing has changed about how I think about you. Nothing."

She glared at him. "Why not? Everybody else is calling me a slut and a whore."

"But you know you're not, so why does the name-calling bother you?"

Layla thought about that. "Because it hurts. And . . . I'm ashamed of what I did."

"Anyone who believes what people are saying don't know the real you."

"And you do?"

"I know what I see," he said, still speaking slowly and calmly.

"What?"

"I see a girl who is all that, but doesn't realize it. A girl who just doesn't get just how awesome she is. A girl who trusted someone she cared about."

"You think you're some kind of shrink?"

"Nope. I'm just a Layla admirer."

"You're probably the only one left in the universe."

"That's fine by me!"

"I had no idea he'd send out those pictures," Layla admitted, struggling to keep her voice steady. "Actually, when he took them, I didn't even consider what could happen if they got out."

"He probably didn't either."

"We were both kinda happy that night. To tell the truth, I wasn't thinking about anything at all."

"Layla, look at me. You deserve to be happy."

"There you go, sounding like a shrink again." Layla sighed.

"My bad."

She hesitated, then told him, "Donny told me he loved me—for the very first time."

Justin made no comment.

"So if he loved me, why would he do something to hurt me so badly?"

Justin peered at her in the darkness. "I guess it's partly my bad."

"Why?"

"I clocked him in the hall, remember? In front of everybody."

"True that. But he didn't go after you; he decided to hurt me instead."

"He lashed out the only way he could, 'cause he knows he can't beat me!"

"Yeah, right. You better watch your back. Donovan fights dirty."

"I can handle him if I need to." Justin paused. "But we both got three days' suspension. I'm supposed to be heading home now." He gently reached out and touched her hand. "I'd fight for you again, Layla."

"Seriously?"

"I've heard them whispering in the hall too. The next person who talks down to you will have to deal with me."

She shook her head. "You'd end up fighting the whole school, and be kicked out the rest of the year. This thing is huge. And nasty."

"All I need to do is wipe the floor with two or three of them. They'll shut up."

"You're a really good guy, you know that?"

"That's what my mom used to tell me," he said, glancing away for a moment.

"Hey, you know what? My dad came home last night."

"How was it?" he asked, his attention instantly back to her.

"A little awkward at first. I was ten when he got locked up. So much has happened since then—there's a whole lot of territory to cover."

"How's your mom handling it?"

"Better than I thought she would. I figured she'd leave him on the sidewalk. But I think she's glad he's back. I think she wants to try, at least."

"Well, that's good, right?"

"But what if my parents find out about this mess, Justin?"

"I hate to say it, but they probably will, ya know. You might want to tell them yourself rather than let it trickle down to them through the Internet."

"Why did he do this to me? Why? It will break my father's heart. He still calls me his little princess. Can you believe it?"

"What about your mom?"

"Oh, man! I don't even want to think about it! She'll holler and yell, but I think she'll be more disappointed than angry."

"Do you want me to go with you?"

"You would do that?"

"Yeah, I would. I want your dad to know that not all dudes are simply after his daughter's underwear."

"You're not?" She grinned at Justin.

"Nope. I just want to dance with you. Forever."

Justin and Layla sat quietly in the darkness of the auditorium, but for the first time in a long time, Layla was beginning to see a bit of light.

39

DIAMOND, *Thursday, April 18   9 p.m.*

"There is danger in the air for you tonight."

—from *Peter Pan*

Thane left the dinner tray as usual that night. A hamburger, fries, and amazingly, a Wendy's frosty. The sweet coolness of the treat made her cry as she licked the spoon.

A spoon.

A spoon! She quickly tucked it under the pillow, and hoped against hope that Thane wouldn't notice it was not under the pile of wrappers and napkins on the tray.

Diamond longed for one of her mother's home-cooked

meals. She promised herself she'd eat meatloaf, even peas and lima beans, just to be in her mother's kitchen once more.

Twenty minutes later, Thane took the tray without comment, leaving the usual bottle of drug-laced water and locking the door behind him. Diamond took the water to the bathroom and poured it out, refilled the bottle with tap water and drank that. Then she grabbed the spoon and squeezed the bowl of it in half. It snapped onto a perfect point.

She looked up at the small window. The little bit of sky she could see was leaden with clouds. The wind blew in sudden gusts, shaking the attic room.

For the first time in many nights, Diamond's head felt clear, but the dread of what was to come never went away. She begged the Lord to give her strength to endure another night. She had to get out of here!

When the film crew arrived and connected the cameras to the tripods, she pretended to be asleep. It took all her effort not to cringe as they touched her, removed her clothes, and positioned her. They no longer tied her arms to the bed.

"Ah, still so lovely," she heard Thane say. "Cameras ready?"

"Ready, sir," said the voice of one of the cameramen.

Thunder rumbled in the distance.

Thane leaned over Diamond, saying "Smile, my sweet. This is your audition tape that will take you to the next level, so let's dedicate this evening to Shasta."

Diamond tried not to recoil at his touch, tried not to

gag from the smell of Thane's sickly sweet cologne, his hot breath on her face.

More thunder. Louder. More insistent. Sharp streaks of lightning flickered through the window above her head.

Diamond pretended to stir, moan, and stretch. She extended one arm upward, ever so gradually. She reached under the pillow. She grabbed the shard of the spoon. It was time.

As fast and as fiercely as she could, she swung her arm down and pushed with all her might, stabbing Thane just above his shoulder blades.

Thane screamed and scrambled backward, grabbing his bleeding neck. That was all Diamond needed. Stark naked, she darted toward the unlocked door.

She knew she had only seconds before he got over the shock and they came after her. She dashed down one winding flight of stairs, then another, then another. Dizzy with fear, she raced to the huge front door. *Oh, please be unlocked!* She figured with customers coming in and out, Thane might be less careful about locks and alarms.

She pulled on the latch. Nothing. She pulled again. Nothing. She heard footsteps thudding behind her. She gave one full, final tug, and, oh thank God, the door swung open.

There was no time to think. She just ran. And ran. She recalled the driveway was incredibly long, so she figured she'd be safer in the woods. Lightning flashed, illuminating the sky, and thunder exploded all around her. Diamond sprinted away from the house and toward the streetlights she saw far off in the distance.

She heard a noise behind her, but didn't stop to look—she just ran faster. But the sound was closer, gaining. Diamond's heart thudded—they couldn't catch her now. She pushed on harder. Please, no!

Then, to her amazement, she realized that Bella was right beside her. The dog pulled ahead. Her coat was soaked, her feet were muddy, but she bounded just ahead of Diamond as if the run were designed for her pleasure, darting over fallen trees, switching to clearer paths, almost as if she were leading the way.

Diamond stole a quick glance behind her. The two cameramen were in pursuit. Thane was right behind them. The cameramen were overweight, and she was sure she'd be able to keep them outdistanced. Thane, however, was running like a demon, and soon overtook his men.

Run, Diamond, run! she repeated, like a prayer. *Run, Diamond, run!* She followed the dog. Sticks bit into her bare feet. The wind increased, sending branches whipping against her arms, her chest. Rain pelted her, running down her naked body.

Another streak of lightning pierced the sky. She glanced behind her again. The cameramen were no longer in sight. But Thane was getting closer. Between rolling explosions of thunder, she could hear Thane crashing through the woods after her.

Diamond gasped for breath, her chest aching for air. She felt as if the whole world were shaking with noise and power. Lightning webbed the sky. Thunder cracked.

And still she ran, terrified that Thane would catch her.

Gulping and heaving, she was trying to figure out which way to go when Bella circled back around to her . . . and nudged her to keep going. Diamond dashed after her, zigzagging through the woods, following the soaked dog, and checking behind her when she could. A huge bolt of lightning brightened the sky, and Diamond stopped short.

A four-foot ditch loomed directly in front of her. She couldn't tell how deep it was, but she had no chance to change direction. Thane was only a few yards behind her.

Bella didn't hesitate. She leaped the ditch effortlessly, then turned toward Diamond, willing her to follow.

Diamond took a deep breath and did what she'd done a hundred times on the dance floor—leaped into the air and across the gulf. Her bare feet screamed in pain as she touched down, but she'd made it to the other side of the ditch. She reached for the dog like a talisman, and glanced behind her as the sky lit up again.

Thane, his face red and furious, was also attempting to jump the ditch.

He didn't make it.

His scream erupted in the darkness. It was the deep, agonizing cry of an animal in extreme pain. Another thunderclap, farther away now. Another scream.

"Help me!" Thane cried out in the darkness.

Diamond hesitated.

"My leg—I think my leg is broken. Help me, please!"

Diamond peeked back into the ditch. In the next brief torch of lightning, she could see him. Thane lay flat, his right arm impaled by the sharp branch of a tree, his left leg twisted at an unnatural angle. The next flash of lightning showed that, yes, a large shard of broken bone protruded from his thigh.

"Please, Diamond," he begged. "If you help me, I'll take you home, and our little adventure can be forgiven and forgotten."

Diamond thought back to the horrors of the past few days. Then she recalled all she'd learned in church about forgiveness. She leaned over the ditch.

The wind was slowly subsiding. Diamond barely noticed the rain. Another flash of lightning showed Thane moaning, blood now pouring from his leg.

Carefully, Diamond lowered herself down to where Thane lay.

He looked up at her beseechingly. "I knew you'd help me. I knew you were special from the moment I first saw you, Diamond."

She touched his slacks, near the pocket.

"It wasn't all that bad, was it?" Thane whimpered. "I'll make it up to you—I've got money—lots of it. I'd planned to pay you all along. You deserve it."

Diamond didn't say a word as she reached quickly into Thane's pants pocket. The moment she grabbed his cell phone, she scrambled out of the ditch and away from him, elation flooding her.

"I hope you rot in Hell!" she finally screamed at him.

The rain had slowed to a soft drizzle, and the wind had lost its fury. The thunder rumbled only in the distance.

Diamond trembled as she punched in the first phone

number she had ever memorized. The dog huddled close.

"Hello?"

When she heard her mother's voice, Diamond could barely speak beyond the gasps and gulps of tears.

"Mom?"

"Diamond? Diamond?" Her mother began to shriek. "It's Diamond! It's Diamond! It's Diamond, honey! Where are you? Oh, Diamond, I knew you'd be alive. Where are you? Where are you?" Now her mother was sobbing.

"I'm not sure where I am, but please come get me. Please hurry! I'm so sorry for all the bad things I've done. Oh, Mom, please come bring me home."

40

LAYLA, *Friday, April 19   9 a.m.*

"I am your friend no more. Begone from me forever."
—from *Peter Pan*

When Mercedes answered the door the next morning, she was still in her pajamas. Layla shivered in a thin jacket, the cool morning air seemingly blowing her into Mercedes' living room. The sky was ruddy, as if struggling to throw off the clouds of past week.

"What's up, girl?" Mercedes asked as Layla tossed her purse to the floor. "You look like you had a rough night."

"It was pretty bad—but nothing compared to Diamond's

night." Layla rubbed her arms and blew on her hands. "I can't believe she escaped. She's back! She's back! She's back!"

"Yeah, awesome, huh? I've been up all night, girl, trying to get information," Mercedes told her, "but there aren't many details yet. Come on up to my room—we gotta talk."

Layla and Mercedes hurried upstairs. Layla pulled a blanket around herself, climbed onto Mercedes' unmade bed, and tried to make her thoughts stand still so she could focus. "This is the second day in less than a week that I've skipped school," Layla admitted.

"My mom actually insisted I stay home today—how 'bout that?" Mercedes told her. "Besides, who could concentrate on Baxson's biology or Senora Sanchez's Spanish? This is life-and-death stuff."

"Yeah. True that."

Both girls checked their phones for messages, but there just weren't many details yet. All the kids kept repeating and resending the same info.

"So they found her *naked* in some woods?" Layla whispered, pulling the blanket close around herself.

"That's all my mom would tell me. She used the dude's cell phone to call her mother, and they used that signal to find her. She must have been terrified out of her mind."

"And totally embarrassed," Layla added, realizing how much she could empathize with Diamond on that part of it. She understood shame. "How'd she get his phone?"

"I'm not exactly sure. Her mother told my mother that she'd been held about five miles from the mall, and she finally escaped by stabbing the guy with a knife or something. I think."

"Oh my God! She stabbed him?"

"In the neck. He sure had it coming."

"You got that right. Who was he?"

"Not sure. But my mom told me the police said he's a known pedophile and this wasn't his first abduction."

Layla huddled under the blanket. "*Abduction.* Even the *sound* of that word makes me gag."

"Yeah, me too. Mom said he was a registered sex offender. In several states. What I don't get is why wasn't he locked up? Why is somebody like that allowed to roam free and hang around malls and stuff?"

"They should make weirdos like that wear T-shirts that say 'Pedophile' in big red letters to warn people off!" Layla agreed angrily.

"Not likely," Mercedes said with a shrug.

"What did he, uh, do to her?" Layla asked carefully.

"The very worst you can imagine. And then some."

"I can't . . . I just can't even make myself think about what she went through," Layla said, pulling the blanket tighter around herself.

"Six days. Six nights."

The two girls sat in silence for a few minutes. Mercedes grabbed the other half of the blanket and tucked it around her feet.

"When we get the chance to talk to her again, we gotta let her know we'll be there for her," Layla said.

"I know," Mercedes replied, "but what do you say to make her feel better? I have no words."

"Maybe I do."

"So, how are *you* holding up, girlfriend?" Mercedes asked Layla.

"Donovan's photos went viral, no shocker there," Layla said sadly. "But it's nothing compared to what Diamond's gone through. I've just got to get over it and move on somehow."

"Compared to Diamond, yeah, but it still sucks scissors, Layla. You have every right to be upset. I'd be crazy mad." She paused, then asked, "Your parents are really pissed, huh?"

"Yeah." Layla tried to smooth a wrinkle on the bedspread. "Somebody showed them to my mother at her job last night. She left in the middle of a shift to come home and yell at me."

"What did you say?"

"Nothing. She'd never understand."

"What did your father say?"

"You know what he did?" Layla looked at Mercedes, her eyes desperate. "He sat in the kitchen and started to cry. Then he ripped down the yellow curtains. That hurt me more than anything. So I locked myself in my room. I left this morning without talking to either of them."

"Hey, the photo stuff is gonna to blow over. People are like dogs fighting over garbage—they'll get bored soon. Besides, I imagine they're probably all gossiping about Diamond now."

Layla shook her head miserably. "Maybe."

"You talk to Donovan?"

"No. I don't plan to waste another breath on him. I just wish I understood how could he do this to me."

"What about Justin?"

Layla felt her cheeks grow warm. "He sent me a text with a picture of some yellow roses. No words, just the roses."

"Nice touch."

"At least he doesn't seem to think I'm trash."

"He never did. I don't think he ever will. And you know what? You can take it slow. He's waited this long—he'll wait until you're ready. That guy really cares about you."

"I'm trying." Layla's phone buzzed, and she jumped, startled. She checked the caller ID, opened it cautiously, and said, "Hi, Daddy."

"Did you sleep well?" he asked.

"Not really."

"I didn't either. You left this morning without saying good-bye," he told her, his voice slightly accusing.

"I'm so sorry, Daddy," she blurted out. "I've been looking forward to you coming home for so long, and I had to mess it up."

Her father paused. "Layla, I was up all night thinking, and I realized it's not you I'm upset with—it's that animal who texted those pictures!"

Layla choked back a sob.

"Don't cry, Layla. I gotta take a little bit of the responsibility too. I shoulda been here for you. I haven't been much of a father," he admitted. "But what that boy did is unforgivable!"

"You know, there was a time when I would have defended him, Daddy, but no more. I'll never let anybody do anything like that to me again."

"Let me tell you something, Layla," her father said, his voice laced with fury. "I just got out that stinkin' orange jumpsuit, but I'd let them put it on me again if I could get my hands on that piece of scum."

"Oh, Daddy, please don't do that! We just got you home, and believe me, Donovan is not worth it. If you do that, he will have managed to hurt *me* again!" Layla spoke in a whoosh. "Can we just start over? Can you forgive me?"

"I already put the curtains back up," her father replied.

Relief spread through Layla's entire body. "Thanks, Daddy," she whispered.

"When are you coming home? And isn't this a school day?"

"I'll explain everything tonight, Dad. I have *so* much to tell you. I love you, Daddy."

"I love you too, Layla. We'll talk more later."

Layla shut her phone off and gave Mercedes a shy smile.

"I could only hear half of that," Mercedes said, "but it sounds like you and your father are gonna patch things up."

"Yeah, I think so. Unless Donovan is unfortunate enough to cross his path. You think the curtains suffered? Oo-wee! He sounded fierce and scary."

"I imagine Diamond's father must feel the same way. Worse! How do you deal with your anger at a monster like the guy who took Diamond?"

"I don't know," Layla admitted. Her phone buzzed

once more. She glanced at it and looked at Mercedes in alarm. "It's Donny! What should I do?"

"Don't answer it!"

The phone kept ringing. Layla raised one eyebrow at Mercedes, then opened the phone and answered angrily. "What do you want, Donovan?"

"Hey, babe."

"I am *not* your babe. I am not your anything!"

"Hey, don't hang up. I, uh, need your help. The cops picked me up."

"Good!"

"No, wait! They're charging me with passing around porn! But you're no porn queen, Layla. They've got it all wrong."

"So you're acting like this is *my* fault? You gotta be kidding!" She stared at Mercedes in disbelief.

"So prove them wrong, my sweet Layla. Prove you're not the whore folks are sayin' you are."

"*What?*"

"Can you bring some money down here? I know you got a little college money saved. I just need ten percent bail—only a thousand dollars. I promise I'll pay you back."

"You ruin *my* reputation, and you want *me* to bail you out of jail?" she screamed into the phone.

"So I guess the slut stories are true."

Layla's voice went hard. "Donovan, listen carefully. I want you to hear this real good. Are you listening?"

"Yeah."

"You are dead to me. Dead, you pissant!" She jabbed

at the off button and looked at Mercedes, her mouth open. "Can you *believe* him?"

"Whew! I gotta say—you told him off good, girl."

For a moment, Layla was so angry she couldn't speak. Finally she told Mercedes that Donny had been arrested.

"What's the charge?" Mercedes asked.

"Something about passing porn. Somebody turned him in!"

"I didn't know you could get pinched for that. Kids send sext messages all the time."

"I guess it's a crime. Who knew?" Layla said.

"I can't believe he wanted you to bring him bail money. He's beyond unbelievable."

"I'm done," Layla replied firmly. "Forever."

"Good for you! 'Cause the Layla of two days ago would have brought him a pound cake with a knife baked in it like they did in those old movies."

"No more. I'm blocking his number from my phone. No, even better, I'll change my number completely."

"'Bout time!" Mercedes pulled out her own phone and checked for text updates about Diamond, but nobody knew anything more. "You think you'll have to go to court?" she asked Layla.

"Maybe. Probably. But I'm not scared of him anymore. I'll tell the truth, even if it's embarrassing." Layla thought for a moment. "Boy, I bet Diamond will have to testify against that animal who took her, you think?"

"I hadn't thought of that—oh, that would be awful, to have to face him again," Mercedes said.

"Yeah, but I bet she'll be glad to see him get locked

up. I think she had to be pretty brave," Layla replied thoughtfully. "What she did took guts. She'll want to see it through."

Mercedes' phone ringing interrupted them. She picked it up immediately. "Oh, Mrs. Landers, how is she doing? We've been crazy worried. I'm here with Layla. Can we come see her? Please? Oh, thanks so much. Yes, I understand. We'll be there in an hour." She looked at Layla nervously. "Diamond's mom is gonna let us see her at the hospital! She says she's asking for us. Let's bounce."

They hurried outside to Mercedes' car. Layla looked up at the clear morning sky. For the first time in over a week, she could see a thin haze of sun behind the clouds.

41

MERCEDES, *Friday, April 19   12 p.m.*

"Wendy, let us go home."
—from *Peter Pan*

Mercedes hated the smell of hospitals—disinfectant and alcohol, tinged with fear. She tiptoed with Layla down the long halls to Room 7719. Outside the door was a handwritten sign that said LANDERS, DIAMOND.

Mercedes grasped Layla's hand as they slowly pushed open the heavy door.

Diamond lay against stark white sheets, her hair loose on the pillow, her face looking small and hollow, with red, welted cuts and scratches across her brow and cheeks. Her wrists were wrapped in thick white gauze, and other smaller bandages dotted her upper arms and her neck. An IV ran into her left arm, tubes snaking up under the blue hospital gown to a couple of bags that dripped clear liquids. Another machine above her bed beeped softly. Her eyes were closed.

Her mother sat in a chair next to her, leaning over the bed and holding Diamond's right hand as if she would never let it go again.

"Hey, girls," Mrs. Landers whispered. "Our Diamond came back to us." She was biting her lips, as if to keep from crying.

Mercedes felt small and scared, like she was six instead of sixteen. Her hands were sweaty, and her mouth felt dry—she wasn't sure if coherent words would even come out of her mouth. But she managed to choke out, "Is she gonna be, like, okay?"

Diamond opened her eyes then and smiled at them. "Yep. I'm gonna be, like, okay." She sounded a little raspy, but it was beyond great to hear her voice.

Mercedes tried not to cry, but she couldn't help it. "We were so scared, so worried," she burbled. "I'm so sorry."

Diamond untangled her right hand from her mother's and touched Mercedes' arm. "Look, girlfriend, what happened is nobody's fault but mine. I can't believe how stupid I was." Her voice got even raspier. "Actually, all of the blame lies directly on that . . . that monster who took me." She squeezed her eyes tightly closed and gripped Mercedes' sweaty hand.

Mercedes tried to imagine what Diamond had gone through, but she just couldn't. All she knew was she had to make Diamond know she was safe forever—with real friends.

"You must be *so* glad to be home," Layla ventured after a moment.

"Yeah, like you wouldn't believe."

"Looks like you got a few, um, scratches there," Mercedes said, not trying to pry, but not wanting to ignore them either.

"Just a few bumps and bruises," Diamond answered. "And I'm starving. That stuff will heal quickly. The rest"— she paused, looking away—"is going to take some time." She let go of Mercedes and reached for her mother.

"You had folks praying for you at church—even at school!" Mercedes said, trying to fill in the awkward silence. "We had a candlelight vigil. It was awesome."

"Wish I coulda seen it," Diamond said with a small smile. "Looks like those prayers worked."

"Where's Shasta?" Mercedes asked.

"My dad just took her home to get some rest. She'd been here since I got here last night. She and my mom have been fighting over who gets to hold my hand."

"Shasta's a brave little cookie."

"She told me she redecorated her room in black Magic Marker," Diamond said with a laugh. "I promised I'll help her repaint it when I get home." Then she added, "Hey, isn't there school today? How did you two get off?"

Mercedes laughed quietly, as if she were afraid to act too cheerful. "You were our excuse," she explained. "Way too much stress to concentrate on Spanish or biology."

"I feel you." She turned to Layla. "How's Donny?"

Layla caught Mercedes' eye for a moment, then said, "Uh, we split up. Permanently. It's a long, really ugly story."

Diamond's eyes filled with sympathy. "I understand ugly. One day we'll have to talk about it."

"Yeah, maybe."

"You and Steve still tight?" Diamond asked Mercedes.

Mercedes couldn't help but smile. "We're good. He still sends me a text every single morning. Sometimes he sends me a song."

"That's great. I need to wrap myself up in as much happy as I can find from now on."

"We can help you there! Let's see," Layla said. "It's finally stopped raining. There's a sale on shoes at Macy's. I'm getting a B in Spanish. How's that for a bit of happy?"

"I got more," Diamond said. "Guess what? I've got a dog!"

"A welcome-home present?" Mercedes asked.

"No. She belonged to, uh, the man who took me." She paused to collect herself. "But Bella—that's the dog—she's an Irish setter—stayed with me every afternoon; she's the only thing that kept me from losing my mind. I think she even helped me when I was running away."

"So how did you get her home?" Layla asked.

"Well, the life squad and Daddy and Mom got to the place where I'd been held about the same time. I was halfway hysterical, but I made Daddy put her in our car before they took me away."

"So where is she now?"

"She waited patiently in the car the whole time the doctors were taking care of me. Daddy and Shasta took her home. That dog helped save my life. I couldn't leave her alone in the rain."

"That's incredible," Layla said.

"You say her name is Bella?" Mercedes asked.

"For now. But I think I'm going to change it to Pixie or Tutu or something. I'm gonna let Shasta help me."

Miss Ginger burst into the room then, her hair a mess as usual, a bouquet of pansies and daisies in her hand. "Oh, Diamond! Oh, Diamond!" was all she could say. Mercedes could tell she was having trouble holding back her tears.

"Hey, Miss G."

"It's so wonderful to see you—so, so wonderful! We were all so worried and frightened."

"I think I'm gonna be fine, Miss G. And my dance training even kicked in while I was running in the woods," Diamond said proudly. "You shoulda seen the ditch I leaped over. Best grand jeté ever! I guess I have you to thank for all that practice."

"You don't know how good that makes me feel. I'm gonna work everybody a little harder tonight, in your honor," she said in a half-teasing voice.

"Thanks so much for coming," Mrs. Landers said to Miss Ginger. "This means the world to her."

"You couldn't have kept me away," Miss Ginger replied, turning to Diamond's mother. "I know you're exhausted. Try to get some rest now that she's back."

"I'll sleep soundly tonight, that's for sure," Mrs. Landers answered.

Miss Ginger turned to Layla and said with eyebrows raised, "Skipping school again, Miss Layla?"

"I promise, never again, Miss G.," Layla said earnestly. "But I just had to see Diamond."

"I understand that. I canceled my class of senior citizens who take tango lessons, so we're even. But you get your butt back in class on Monday."

"Yes, ma'am," Layla said. "I promise."

Miss Ginger looked at Layla with steely eyes. "And did you resolve that problem we talked about?"

Layla returned her teacher's gaze. "Absolutely. It is over, and I am taking charge of *me* for a change."

"Excellent!" Turning to Mercedes, Miss Ginger said, "I expect you both in class tonight—on time. We'll have a wonderful celebration at the studio."

"What's been going on at the studio?" Diamond asked.

"We've started practicing for *Peter Pan*, but you take your time and come back whenever you feel you're ready. A part in the show will be waiting for you if you want it."

"Thanks, Miss Ginger," Diamond whispered.

"We did a sort of 'Dance for Diamond' session a couple of days ago," Mercedes told her. "Everybody sorta danced what they felt. It was stupid fresh."

"It was powerful dance therapy," Miss Ginger explained. "And it was Zizi's idea!"

"I did a pas de deux with Justin," Layla said with a mischievous smile. "It was fun. I guess that's another piece of happy!"

Mercedes rolled her eyes. "Talk about dance therapy! The dude is crazy for Layla, and she's, like, clueless!"

"I'm starting to get it," Layla admitted with a smirk.

Miss Ginger gave Layla a big hug. Then she leaned over and told Diamond, "There is nothing stronger than a diamond, my dear. Welcome home." She gave Diamond a quick kiss on the cheek and breezed out of the room.

"I missed Miss Ginger," Diamond admitted. "I missed all of you. I dreamed of dancing while I was locked in that room." She looked away, toward the window.

"When do you think you'll come back to school or dance class?" Layla asked.

"Not for a while," Diamond's mother replied. "We want to give her time to heal physically as well as emotionally. Plus, she needs time to eat piles and piles of her mama's turkey and gravy."

"And ice cream," Diamond said. "I want a gallon of butter pecan ice cream."

"We shoulda brought you some," Mercedes said. "But we didn't know how you'd, uh, be . . ."

"It's okay," Diamond said, filling in the empty air. "You know, I never woulda thought that I'd want to cuddle with my mother all day. But that's where I am."

Her mom reached over and smoothed Diamond's hair.

"Hey, I didn't tell you—my dad came home," Layla said.

"Oh, that's awesome," Diamond said. "You two probably have lots of catching up to do."

"Yeah. It's not all pretty, but I guess we'll survive."

"You know, it's gonna take me a year just to recuperate

from the millions of questions the police asked me," Diamond said, closing her eyes once more. "Over and over—the same questions."

"Did they catch the guy?" Mercedes asked, wondering how she hadn't thought to ask that yet.

"Oh, yeah. He was pretty busted up—I know he at least had a broken leg and a bloody arm—and one of the policemen told me he was taken to a hospital in handcuffs."

"Not this one?" Layla asked, looking around nervously.

"That was one of the first things I asked!" Diamond replied. "He's way across town. On his way to prison."

"Will you have to go to court to testify?" Mercedes asked.

"Yeah, eventually. These things take a while, the cops said, but probably so. I'm not afraid to face him. I intend to tell every nasty little detail of what he did to me." She narrowed her eyes. "I want him in jail for the rest of his life, so that no other girl will have to go through what I did."

"I don't think I could have made it," Mercedes admitted, taking up Diamond's hand again.

"Yeah, you would have. I guess you just do what you have to do," Diamond said. "He's done this before, can you believe it? In other cities." She paused. "There are videotapes on the Internet. Of *everything* he's done," she added slowly.

"I'll be right there by your side, Diamond," Mercedes exclaimed as she figured out exactly what Diamond meant.

"We all will," Layla said. "Especially me. I'll tell you all about my little adventures while you were gone when you're stronger."

Mrs. Landers stood up and began tucking the blanket more tightly around Diamond. "Thank you girls for coming, but I want Diamond to get her rest now. You can come back and visit when she comes home, okay?"

Mercedes and Layla each gave Diamond a hug, whispered their good-byes, and left the room.

Halfway down the hall, Mercedes leaned against a wall and eased down to the polished floor, collapsing in huge gulps of tears. Layla sat beside her and cried just as hard.

42

DIAMOND, *Three Weeks Later   Saturday, May 11   2 p.m.*

"This ought not to be written in ink but in a golden splash."
—from *Peter Pan*

Diamond opened the door to the Crystal Pointe Dance Academy, walked into the main dance room, and inhaled deeply. It smelled of cocoa and costumes, of perspiration and popcorn, of happiness and hope. *Happy smells a lot like leftover sweat,* she thought with a smile. The room was silent, and Diamond stood very still. She could *feel* the music she'd missed, as if the rhythms hovered just beyond her ability to recall. She visualized every single movement, leap, and twist, every single chorus and lyric and song. She felt a little trembly.

Miss Ginger touched her arm gently, and Diamond, startled, jumped.

"I didn't mean to frighten you," Miss Ginger said gently.

"I was just remembering the music," Diamond explained. "Remembering everything."

"Take your time. Walk around. Let all the good memories come back slowly," Miss Ginger told her.

"I love this place," Diamond said, breathing deeply once more. "The dance posters, the sheer curtains in the windows, that ridiculously beautiful chandelier. It's like coming home."

"You know what they say—home is where you feel loved," Miss Ginger replied with a knowing nod.

Diamond dropped her dance bag to the floor and looked around, as if seeing the place for the first time. The lumpy spot on the marley floor. The small crack in the far right mirror. The red paint spots that had dripped on the white wall last summer during a fix-up party. The ballet barres, well worn in the middle. The costumes on display upstairs. The trophies, dusty in the display case.

"Thanks for letting me come in alone, Miss Ginger," Diamond said finally. "I don't think I'm ready to face the whole group yet."

"I understand completely," Miss Ginger said.

"I danced in my head a lot while I was, uh, gone," Diamond said.

"Did it help?"

"Yeah. Helped keep me from going crazy, I guess," Diamond admitted.

"Are you ready to hear some music?" Miss Ginger asked.

"In a minute. Can I ask you something first?" Diamond took off her tennis shoes and slid the familiar pointe shoes onto her feet.

"Sure."

"Do you think I'll ever be normal again?"

Miss Ginger took a moment before answering. "Nothing will ever be exactly the same," she said finally, honestly. "But maybe normal is not the word you're looking for. You're a gifted dancer. You're a loving daughter and sister. You're an outstanding student. Why lower your standards to just plain normal?"

Diamond frowned. "You know what I mean."

"I know you can focus on the past and let it destroy you, or you can focus on the future and let it lift you up. It's your choice, Diamond."

"I still have really bad dreams."

"Of course you do! But, in time, they will fade. Your mom told me you were seeing a professional counselor, right?"

"Yeah. She's nice. And I guess she's helping a little. It's too soon to tell." Diamond grinned then. "But she can't dance."

"Let's get some music going then, okay?"

"Can you play 'Faith' by Jordin Sparks?" Diamond asked.

"Great choice," Miss Ginger replied. "Ready?"

Diamond nodded.

The piano plaintively plinked out the intro, and Diamond moved to the center of the empty room and just listened to the words as the piece swelled to its completion. Miss Ginger hit PLAY again. The song was about sad eyes, stolen smiles, and dark, dark skies. But the song was most powerful when Jordin sang about seeing the stars, about having faith— *"When you fall the hardest, you find how strong you are . . ."* The song began for the third time.

Then, gradually, slowly, Diamond began to dance. Her body echoed her pain and agony as she moved across the room, the heavy-toed pointe shoes barely making a sound as she embraced the music. She didn't look at herself in the mirror as she spun around, balancing on one foot and using her free leg and her arms to propel herself around in a whipping motion until she was dizzy. She twisted and swayed. She let the tears fall.

Finally, Diamond lifted herself up in a relevé, a smooth continuous rise onto her toes. She was looking at the ceiling, but reaching for the sky—forever, finally rising above it all. She balanced on one foot, then slowly slid the other leg up, up, up. She lifted that leg as if it were weightless, stretching it, stretching it, her body an arrow of beauty.

Then, ever so slowly, she rolled out of the extension and dropped gracefully to a sitting position on the floor. The song reached its conclusion, and Diamond sat there, taking deep silent breaths. The song played one more time, echoing against the walls.

When it ended, she looked up at her teacher. "I want to dance again," she said emphatically. "I want to dance forever."

Songs Used

"Beat It" by Michael Jackson

"Candyman" by Christina Aguilera

"Butterfly" by Mariah Carey

"Almost There" from the movie *The Princess and the Frog*

"Boom Boom Pow" by The Black Eyed Peas

"Rumour Has It" by Adele

"Tender Shepherd" from the Mary Martin version of *Peter Pan*

"Where Do Broken Hearts Go?" by Whitney Houston

"Tick Tock" from the movie *Sherlock Holmes: A Game of Shadows*

"Everybody Hurts" by Avril Lavigne
"Mirror" by Monica
"Sister" by Cris Williamson
"Firework" by Katy Perry
"Bluebird" by Sara Bareilles
"Beautiful Flower" by India.Arie
"Black Butterfly" by Deniece Williams
"Heaven & Earth" by Kelly Rowland
"Dance of the Swans" from Tchaikovsky's *Swan Lake*
"Kiss Kiss" by Chris Brown
"Just the Way You Are" by Boyce Avenue
"Agony" from the Broadway musical *Into the Woods*
"Faith" by Jordin Sparks